WINTER'S CRIMES 13

WINTER'S CRIMES 13

Edited by George Hardinge

Macmillan

ISBN 0 333 31831 5

First published 1981 by
MACMILLAN LONDON LIMITED
London and Basingstoke
Associated companies in Auckland, Dallas, Delhi,
Dublin, Hong Kong, Johannesburg, Lagos, Manzini, Melbourne,
Nairobi, New York, Singapore, Tokyo,
Washington and Zaria

Typeset in Great Britain by
MB GRAPHIC SERVICES
Bovingdon, Hertfordshire

Printed in Great Britain by
THE ANCHOR PRESS LIMITED
Tiptree, Essex

Bound in Great Britain by
WM. BRENDON AND SON LIMITED
Tiptree, Essex

Contents

EDITOR'S NOTE

The policy of *Winter's Crimes* anthologies is to publish new short stories – written specially for the series – that will never before have seen the light of day except possibly in America.

As *Winter's Crimes* reaches the age of thirteen its companion volume, *Winter's Tales*, appears for the twenty-seventh time, edited by Edward Leeson.

Winter's Crimes has been lucky all the way with its contributors, and the luck holds and grows. I am very grateful to the authors who contributed to this volume, and I do not need to speak for them, since their names are well known.

George Hardinge

Lionel Davidson

INDIAN ROPE TRICK

The Spey is one of the greatest of the great Scottish east coast rivers. Its rate of flow is the fastest of any major river in the United Kingdom. Below Grantown it begins to swell into a big river flowing mostly through a dramatic and precipitous valley where it rushes and boils between a mixture of boulders and sandbanks.

Bang on, thought Waring. That was exactly what it was doing. He could hear it. He was sitting and reading about it. He was doing this in a comfortable chair, in a comfortable lounge, some hundreds of yards from where the boiling and rushing was going on. Even at this distance the tumult of the mighty river was like an engine in the air. It excited him. He sensed great salmon beating up it, in darkness, in snow. *And doing it right now.* Right now Waring wanted to go out in the dark and see them.

However, he didn't. It was months since his operation but he still tired easily. He took a sip of whisky instead; an extra big sip.

'Darling,' his wife said warningly.

'Don't fuss.'

'Your heart will race.'

'Nag.' But he laid whisky and book aside. 'They do it to one,' he told Nigel.

'They want to hang on to one,' Nigel said.

Nigel looked sleepy; contentedly sleepy. Nigel had fished the Blackrock today and got three fine springers;

now sacked and ready for smoking in Aberdeen. Waring had fished the smaller pool and had got nothing. His turn for the Blackrock tomorrow!

Again the sound of the river excited him and again he wanted to go out in the dark to it.

'What I wouldn't mind having a dab at in the morning,' he said to Estelle, 'is the Indian rope trick. If you feel up to it.'

'If *you're* up to it, and the river's up to it.'

'It's what I'd like,' he said.

'Brucie won't,' Nigel said.

'Bugger Brucie.'

'Brucie rules.' Brucie was the gillie.

'Not on our beat.'

Nigel's beat, actually. A beautiful little beat, two rods, syndicate water. By chance Nigel had managed to buy into it years before. The firm had held the syndicate covered against legal costs arising from accidents. When the scion of a tobacco family had managed to drown himself in the Blackrock Nigel had handled the matter and had been in a position to jump the queue and buy the scion's water; for the first two weeks of April. They had been coming up every year since.

'If the snow keeps up,' Estelle said, 'won't it do something to the water? Then there'll be no tricks of any kind.'

'Not this snow,' Waring said. 'It's settling.' But he didn't mind what it did. Snow-melt, peat-stain. He looked forward to using some big gaudy flies in it. A Thunder-and-Lightning, a flashy great Childers. Above all he looked forward to the Indian rope trick.

He felt very happy.

He felt happy just looking forward. Months ago there had been nothing to look forward to. Yet he hadn't minded. In this incredible year he had learned an incredible thing. Dying, he found that though he enjoyed what he had, he didn't mind seeing it all go. It was easy to die; everybody did it; a common affair. But now he had his life back he liked it. He appreciated it more. He appreciated his wife Estelle, and her great qualities. With this year's huge bills and the unlikelihood of his working much longer, his appreciation had rocketed. Estelle's main great quality was her thirty thousand a year.

He had never really lied about it. She knew he didn't love her in the way that she wished to be loved. But she loved *him*. That was the main thing. And he had denied her nothing, while able. He had early discovered another curious truth. Sexually unattractive women were very big on sex. Dame Nature seemed to make them so: some fine adjustment perhaps in the handicapping before the great race for renewal. Whatever the reason, Estelle was certainly a tigress at it. She enjoyed it awfully.

Pondering this, he looked round the big hotel room and wondered if anyone could guess at the jumbo appetites in his smallish plain wife. The room was full of bores all yawning away at their own potty wives, so he looked away again in case one of them should come and talk to him.

He looked at Nigel and caught him having the most enormous yawn himself. All of Nigel was yawning, from the tips of his outstretched fingers right down to his feet. One of these feet, Waring noticed, was close to Estelle's. He had an impression that moments before it had been touching; also that Nigel's tremendous stretching of himself had less to do with actual weariness than with a kind of limbering-up.

Okay, Waring thought. Situation under control. Much less okay would have been a situation not under control, one that he didn't even know about. This one he knew all about.

He had an idea that Estelle had actually wanted to tell him: to explain that it didn't *matter;* that it was just something she had to do; that he was the one she loved and cherished. And he would have been glad if she had said this because he knew she always spoke truthfully.

However, she hadn't said it, and in the tricky situation he couldn't help her to say it. In any case, though she might think it true now, he knew it wouldn't go on being true.

He knew a tremendous amount lately. Since his brush with death he seemed to know practically everything. He felt special knowledge of the imperatives of life, of the programmes laid down for all the living.

Lying in hospital, his life slipping away, he had watched all the people coming and going; coming and going so seriously about their business. He had watched as if from the wrong end of a telescope, and he thought what a silly game! He had enjoyed the game while playing it but he saw that it had no meaning. With his life restored, the joy of the game had returned. What had brought back meaning to the game? He didn't know. Yet mysteriously it was back. Its imperative was back – the same imperative that brought the salmon back, every year, to this river.

The great fish came battling in from the sea, from thousands of miles away, to find just this estuary, just this river, and struggle up it (through rapids, through waterfalls), to spawn where they themselves had been spawned. They couldn't help it, couldn't stop it, had to do it.

As with Estelle: who also had to do what she was doing. Perhaps she thought it just a passing affair; and perhaps it would have been. Except that on this trip, he had seen most plainly, she was growing fond of Nigel. And Nigel was evidently meeting her needs in bed. There was not much doing with *him* in the bed line lately; nothing at all, of course, during his illness, and very little since. He knew each night, after his sleeping draught, that she slipped out to Nigel's room, and he didn't grudge her. But he saw what would come of it.

12

Estelle was not a woman to go chasing after men. But Nigel didn't need chasing. He was there, and an old friend; and one who had been showing signs lately of wanting to settle down himself. Yes, he could see it all coming. She had a *need* for sex, and a dislike of deception. She would want to regularise her life, and slowly a dissatisfaction with him would grow. She loved him now; he didn't doubt it. As Nigel had said, she certainly wanted to hang on to him. She didn't know herself the blind force, the life imperative, that would at first weaken and then destroy the tie between them. But Waring knew. He knew such a lot now.

He was honest with himself and knew that if he had to choose between Estelle and her thirty thousand he would go for the thirty thousand; even if it meant the sad demise of Estelle. But he did not have this choice. Estelle's money was life money. No Estelle, no money.

He thought the best formula would be for Nigel to go and get a wife himself, preferably one who also had thirty thousand of her own. But he knew Nigel was indolent and probably wouldn't. So he had lately revised the formula to a more abbreviated and manageable one.

Nigel would simply have to go.

Estelle had been picking up her knitting, and they were now walking through the lounge, offering cheerful good-nights to those remaining.

Outside he could hear the muffled thudding of the river. It was going like an engine: rushing, boiling. His heart raced, but he didn't mind. Indian rope trick tomorrow!

It was still dark after breakfast, and still a few minutes early, but Brucie was already waiting. He was waiting in the vestibule; standing like a tree in it, smoking his pipe. He had the carrier's note for the Aberdeen salmon-smokers.

13

'Morning, Brucie,' Nigel said, taking the note with pleasure. 'How's the water?'

'High,' Brucie said.

'Fishable?'

'A touch colour.'

'Is it cold?' Estelle said, shivering.

'Healthy,' Brucie said, and took his pipe out.

Estelle tightened the leather belt round her fur coat and pulled her hat over her ears. She knew Brucie meant germs would not survive such healthy conditions.

Brucie had removed his pipe to stare curiously at the coil of rope Waring was carrying. For a moment Waring almost explained. Then he remembered and thought Bugger Brucie, and led the way himself out to the car.

Brucie had de-snowed the car, but with all their breaths and his pipe going it misted up at once. Nigel turned everything on, engine, headlamps, wipers, blower, and in a mild uproar and fuggy discomfort they circled the wide gravel and went slowly out into the village.

The indigo light was paling into a kind of gunmetal. Snow lay everywhere and a few flakes still drifted in the air. Behind them other headlamps swung out of the hotel and turned away.

Nigel kept slowly on, through the village, and out of it, and up, and up, to the hut.

They parked a couple of hundred yards from the hut, and walked up to it through the undergrowth. The chimney was already smoking in the hut. Brucie didn't live in the place but left various bits of gear more or less permanently outside. He left them quite untended, knowing no hand dare touch them. His own ham-like hands were known in the vicinity. For the same reason he never bothered locking the hut. He just went right at it now and pushed the door in without a word. He was offended at Waring for not explaining the rope.

An oil-lamp was burning in the hut and the kettle was singing on the side of the wood stove. By old routine Estelle made the tea while Brucie assembled the tackle and the two men got into their wading gear.

The chest waders, of a rubberised fabric, were stiff and unwieldy, iron cold to the touch. Waring took his shoes off and stepped into his and drew it up to his chest and slipped the braces over his shoulders. Then he sat down and pulled on his heavy woollen stockings and his nailed boots. He felt tired. He sat and drank his tea and watched Brucie continuing to assemble the tackle.

Brucie laid the two fly rods and the two spinning rods on the floor and went out and looked at the water. Then he came back and described it and asked what flies they wanted to use. He did this without expression (and without any mention of spinners, which he abjured); and when they had made their suggestions he told them what to use.

Waring barely listened to him. He had caught him looking at the rope again. He wondered if there was a rule against it. There were rules for practically everything. The bugger might well produce a rule or run off and phone somebody for one. He did not think there could be one; but he didn't know so he kept quiet. He thought he'd first get the rope in the water and then outface Brucie if problems arose. The position for Brucie to be in was of one obeying orders and not giving rulings or tendering opinions. It was important that Brucie should immediately do as he was told when Waring told him the important thing he had to do. He didn't think that Brucie's pride in its present state of offence would allow him to ask about the rope.

Brucie didn't ask about the rope, and he continued being offended. When they left the hut he picked up Nigel's tackle and went straight down with him to the small pool, leaving Waring to carry his own.

Waring didn't mind. With Estelle he collected the gear and they started the long walk down to the Blackrock.

Outside the hut everything was very beautiful. The snowbank was beautiful, and the trees, and the jagged broken valley of the river. The river was immensely beautiful. The air was now totally full of the sound of it, its force and vibration so shattering that Waring laughed out loud. He saw Estelle smiling herself, though her face was pinched with cold.

'You'll warm up!' he called in her ear.

'I'm warm. Let me carry the rope.'

'You're carrying enough.' He had the rope round his neck.

'You're not really going in with it today?'

'I'll see,' he said.

The water was so high he didn't know if he'd get in at all. It was reddish brown, and going fast. But when they reached the bank he saw it was possible. Five or six feet of beach were still exposed. The fingers of shingle were exposed. The fingers ran out to the stream, and he knew the ground on both sides, and it was not deep. Even where it deepened, it wasn't dangerous. It was a question of keeping his footing.

He shook out the rope and slipped the bight over his head.

'Henry, it's dangerous,' Estelle said.

'Don't fuss.'

'The water's much too fast.'

'You'll guide me out.' He tightened the rope under his shoulders. 'I'll wave to you. I'll blow my little whistle.' He dangled the whistle at her from its lanyard, having to shout now, unable to stop laughing. He saw she was laughing herself; lips puckered in alarm but laughing. It was the water. It was the astounding flood of water, endlessly rounding the Blackrock; spume-flecked, magnificent, spray smacking the air. A world of water, and in the water the salmon, wild things in from the sea.

'I'll try the fly,' he said.

Brucie had already put on a fly, a big sunk one.

'Don't, Henry.'

'Just a cast or two.'

'Henry, I'm asking you.'

'And don't pull. You don't have to pull,' he said. 'It's only to guide me back.' But she couldn't hear him now. He was walking cumbrously out along the spit, rod in his left hand and gaff in the right. He used the gaff as a wading stick and came cautiously down off the spit, and took a step, and a few more, and right away knew it was dangerous. The river bed had changed. The water was quite suddenly over his knees, his waist. Even despite the evidence of his eyes he was shocked by the force of it.

He struggled to keep his balance, leaning hard on the gaff. The rod was almost torn from his hand, the long whippy length of it wrenching and thrumming in the water. He managed to lift it and edge farther out, feeling for level footing. He was confused and deafened by the uproar, by the dizzying race of foam. He didn't know how far he'd gone, and daren't turn to see. A backward glance would unbalance him, would have the water up over the top of his chest waders, filling them, sinking him. It had happened to the tobacco man.

He found rock, a solid boulder, and wedged his feet there, leaning against the current. The breath was almost battered out of him. He knew he had to turn and go. He had to do it immediately. His heart was thumping, head spinning with vertigo from the racing water. He closed his eyes against it, planning the moves. But just as he opened them again a salmon leaped. It leaped clean out of the spray, not ten yards from him. 'Oh, my God,' he said. It was big as a big dog, thirty or forty pounds at least. In the air the salmon looked at him. Its cold eye watched him all the way through its long arc until it re-entered the river.

Waring saw where it entered and knew why it had leapt. It had leapt the long ridge of rock that formed one wall of the pool. The salmon was now in the pool. Dozens of other salmon would be there with it, resting before the next onslaught up river.

'Jesus,' he said, and knew he would have to try. He would have just one try. His vertigo had gone suddenly, and he had got the feel of the current. He thought if he was careful he could stand unaided. He tried it and he could. He released the fly from its ring, stripping off line from the reel. He stripped four or five yards off, and raised the big rod double-handed, and got it swishing there and back till he had ten, then fifteen yards in the air, and he shot it. He shot it across and down and saw the heavy line snaking out through the spray and the few see-sawing snowflakes, and felt it belly at once as the current took it. He rolled the rod in the air, mending the line on the water, and it came round very fast. He couldn't see the end of the line but he saw the angle change sharply at his rod tip and knew he was over the pool, and that his fly was in it, bobbing down among the salmon. He willed one of them to come and get it and began drawing in line to keep the fly moving. He held a finger on the line to keep contact with the fly. If a salmon took, it would turn away, and as it turned the fly would check in its jaw; and his finger would feel it.

He stood deep in the current, feeling the adrenalin flowing in him. He was barely aware of the battering pressure now. He brought the line in slowly, brought all of it in, and no salmon took, and he thought *once more: just once.* The salmon were there – dozens, scores of them were there! But he knew it was madness, that at any moment vertigo could seize him again. Also there was the

18

rope trick to be attempted, the *Indian* rope trick; and attempted now before Brucie appeared.

The moment he stopped fishing the vertigo hit him again. He stood stock still in the water, steadying himself with the gaff and closed his eyes and slowly turned, and didn't open them till he thought he was facing the beach. He wasn't quite facing it but he saw it there, thirty or forty feet away, and Estelle hopping on it, gesticulating at him. Her face was pink with cold and she was shouting. He couldn't hear her but he waved back, and almost at once tension came on the rope, and he realised she was pulling him in. He didn't want this. He didn't want it! He saw that every gesture counted, and motioned her to stop, but she couldn't understand. He pointed at the black rock, the huge hump that lay at the far side of the beach, and after a moment she nodded, and he began wading there.

All the river was coming at him now and he leaned into it, prodding with the gaff in front. He prodded carefully, finding the holes where boulders had been, where he could drown so easily now. He knew he was sweating heavily. He had to get beyond the black rock, but he made right for it and once there almost kissed it. He hung on to the gaff and hugged the rock tightly. There was just a narrow ledge under him now, and below it the pool, very deep, very dangerous.

He shuffled his way round the ledge, holding the rock with both arms, and found the beach at the other side, smaller than the one he had left; but still exposed.

He came down off the ledge exhausted but still with no time to rest. He laid his rod on the shingle and slipped the bight of rope over his head. He had marked a projection of rock yesterday, and he found it and attached the rope and tightened up. Then he let the slack of the rope go in the water and saw the current take it. He watched a moment and bent and felt it. The rope was thrumming in the water, but far away at the other end he could still feel Estelle, as he had felt the fly. Indian rope trick. A man went up a rope, and the rope stayed up. Was the man still at the end of the rope? Estelle knew he was at the end of this one. He looked at his watch and started counting.

And now he could rest. And he sat on the beach. At the other end of it was another outcrop of rock, quite small, and beyond that sloping shingle. From there it was just uphill and over the top to the position where Nigel would be fishing below; immediately below at the right time. It wasn't the right time yet.

By ten o'clock Nigel would be there, having worked down from the head of the pool. And once there, Nigel would have to remain there: for a good half hour. It was the only way the river could be fished at that point: too deep to wade. It had to be fished up, across and down, all from the same small point. There was no more than a yard of leeway at either side; and wherever Nigel stood in it, Waring could get him. He had already loosened the boulder. The thing must weigh a couple of hundredweight. It was firmly wedged but moveable. Waring had already moved it, and knew he could topple it without great effort. All understandable. Loosened by rain and snow. Not the gillie's fault. Not the angler's. Hazard of the sport.

It had taken him seven minutes yesterday to get there and back from that point to this one. Now he gave it nine, to allow for contingencies.

The nine minutes ticked away, and he got moving. He fixed himself to the rope, picked up his rod and shuffled round the rock again. Estelle was watching most anxiously, and waved at once. He didn't wave back. Brucie hadn't appeared yet, but he might at any moment. He didn't want Brucie to see him coming from the rock.

He put distance between it. He struggled out to midstream. He stayed a full calculated minute watching the water before turning away. Then he waved. Then she pulled.

She pulled too hard. She'd have him over! He hung back on the rope, steadying himself. But the thing was a help. He was desperately tired now, heart thumping, and with double vision in the bargain. He knew he'd never make it if he had to watch the beach and the racing water in between. Guided by the rope he could concentrate on his feet, and in a few minutes was stumbling out.

Brucie was coming down the slope.

'Darling, that was *lunacy!*' Estelle cried.

Waring couldn't speak.

'I thought I'd literally have a *seizure!*'

She was babbling on but he barely heard her; still trying to catch his breath and remove the rope as Brucie arrived.

The giant stared at him open-mouthed. 'You planning to catch a whale?' he said.

Waring didn't answer. Estelle would babble an explanation soon enough. And there were things in store for Brucie yet.

Estelle almost immediately was babbling. 'I told him not to go in, that the water was too fast. The rope's supposed to guide him back. He can't get a fly out far enough since his illness. But he goes so far!'

'Why so?' Brucie said. 'The fly fishes from here.'

'The fly won't fish.'

'It fishes *parfectly.* Mr Clintock fishes the fly.'

'I want the spinner,' Waring said.

'The spinner?' The spinner was guaranteed to unhinge Brucie. 'Why the spinner? It's fly water. They want fly.'

'Take the spinning rod,' Waring said, 'and go to the next pool. I'll join you shortly.'

'They will take fly, Mr Waring,' Brucie said desperately. 'You must give them a chance, sir. You must have patience.'

21

The "Mr Waring, sir" was an advance. And there was no nonsense about the rope: nothing about it frightening fish. There couldn't be a rule about it.

'Don't waste time, Brucie,' Waring said, pressing on. 'Take the spinning rod. Take all the tackle. Don't forget the gaff.'

He made Brucie come and get the gaff. Brucie bit hard on his pipe but he came and got it and stumped off, deranged.

'Henry, it was so dangerous,' Estelle said.

'You did well,' he told her.

'And you were so miserable to Brucie.'

'Brucie *will* do well.'

'I'll have to make it up to him somehow.'

'Easily done.' There was always a reliable way of making it up to Brucie. The flask was in her shoulder bag now. 'Only you don't have to pull so hard,' Waring said. 'The rope does all the work, and it only upsets you.'

'It's nothing to do with the rope.'

'It's everything to do with the rope,' Waring said.

It was a good ten-minute slog to the pool, and Brucie wasn't there when they arrived. The tackle was there, but Brucie himself had gone up to sulk in the hut. From the hut he could view all the beat.

And that was the next thing, Waring thought. Brucie had to be removed from his view of the beat. It was the reason for putting him through his paces today. D-Day would be the day after tomorrow, when Nigel would once more be in position. That was also D for Departure day, for they'd be checking out after lunch. It would give him only the morning to do it. Not that he needed all morning. He needed nine minutes; and Brucie's instant obedience in the nine minutes.

He fished the spinner for an hour without success, then it

began snowing hard. It was still early for elevenses but they went to the hut, and found Nigel there before them. He and Brucie were weighing a ten-pounder.

'Caught on the fly,' said Brucie heavily.

Estelle sweetened the brute with her flask, and soon had him telling of other great malts he had known so that the atmosphere became quite affable.

Waring distanced himself from all the affability.

No toadying, he told himself. Brucie had to be kept in his place. There was a job ahead of Brucie.

The snow kept on till lunch, and afterwards turned to driving sleet; which meant no more fishing for the day. They did the tweed factory instead. They usually did the tweed factory on every visit. This time Waring was distracted half out of his mind.

He stayed that way all through dinner. The wind driving the sleet had risen. He could hear it slamming away outside. He wondered what it would do to tomorrow's fishing; if there would *be* any fishing. On all the beats there were good stations and not so good ones; it accounted for the strict rotation of rods. If the river was not fishable, the rotation was simply held up. But he couldn't have it held up. He had to have the small pool tomorrow so that Nigel would get it the day after: D-Day.

Later on, in the lounge, the wind began fairly howling. It drowned the sound of the river, and he saw the keener anglers about the room anxiously tapping the barometer.

He kept his nerve, drank his whisky, read his book.

The kind of deep whirling water that often lies beyond these banks is the most likely place for a fisherman, encumbered with heavy equipment, to be sucked down and drowned. This is where he must keep his head. Unless help is close to hand and immediately available . . .

He read the passage again, and then once more, almost

faint with longing. The vision it depicted of Nigel on D-Day was so perfect it was almost a prophecy. The deep whirling water was *just* beyond the bank. Nigel would not be keeping his head, not after a boulder had fallen on it. The only help close to hand would be Waring's, which would in no way be available.

Nigel had begun yawning again and Estelle was folding her knitting. Waring finished his whisky and rose.

Let tomorrow be fishable, he thought. Let it be!

He was slow in turning out in the morning so that Estelle went down before him. This gave him an opportunity to be sick in the bathroom. The snow was going horizontally outside. His legs were so weak he thought he'd faint.

He pulled himself together, however; went down, had his porridge, had a kipper, had two cups of coffee.

'I don't know about you,' Nigel said, peering out of the window. 'But it does not look top o' the morning, does it?'

'See what Brucie says.'

'Oh, Brucie,' Estelle said. Brucie had not yet found any conditions unfishable; which was Waring's remaining hope, and the only thing keeping his kipper down. He didn't know for certain but he seemed to recall a rule that stated that the whole rotation of a beat must proceed if any particular member chose to fish his part of it. He thought he was going to be that member. Brucie must have his say, though.

Brucie was waiting in the vestibule, pipe going.

'Well, Brucie,' Nigel said. 'How is it?'

'Fresh,' Brucie said. Beyond the glass panels of the vestibule something very like a tempest seemed to be in progress.

'Is it fishable?' Waring said.

Brucie took his pipe out and paused, causing Waring's heart almost to stop. 'It's no' *un*fishable,' Brucie said. 'It's no' *parfect*,' he amplified. 'There's a breeze.'

The breeze just at that moment very nearly took the door off.

'Will it be so bad down at the small pool?'

'*No-o*,' Brucie said cautiously. 'You have the high bank there. The small pool would be – fishable.'

'I'll fish it,' Waring said.

He said it quickly. Much too quickly. They all stared at him and Nigel burst out laughing. 'You old weasel,' he said. 'You stoat. You fox. You cunning old swine. You want the Blackrock tomorrow, don't you?'

'Well, I – I'm game to try today,' Waring said, toes curling in his shoes.

Nigel's laughter roared on, and even Brucie's broken teeth bared in a grin. 'Silly old sausage,' Nigel said, prodding him affectionately. 'Of course have it tomorrow. I've had the most marvellous bag. Be my guest, Henry.'

'I'm quite prepared to fish today,' Waring said stiffly.

'Oh, Henry,' Estelle said.

'Give it away, old boy! Take your chance on the Blackrock tomorrow if it's okay.'

'Tomorrow will be parfect,' Brucie said.

'Will it?' Waring said.

'Not a doubt. And there's elsewhere today.'

'Where?'

'The distillery,' Brucie said.

'Oh,' Estelle said.

'The Glentorran. If there's a whole *day*.' He'd been trying to sell them the Glentorran for years now; it was forty miles off, too far for an afternoon jaunt.

'Well, it's very big of you, Nigel,' Waring said.

'Nonsense. I've had splendid value this trip.'

So he had, Waring thought, taking one thing with another. 'Okay, then. Fine.'

'Wonderful! Lead on MacBruce.'

Waring quietly glowed in the car; but retained his

caution. There were details to be sewn up yet. His mind roamed over the familiar ones. Fingerprints on boulders. Could there be? But if so, why not? He'd been there many times. *Footprints* in *snow*. Yes. He'd have to work on that; work backwards, obliterating them. And on shingle, the upward path? But who would look? Foul play not suspected. A boulder had gone over, weakened by weather. Unless he dropped something in his excitement: a knife, fishing scissors, any of a dozen bits of paraphernalia he'd have with him. Even his fishing hat. But he'd be using the hat, to brush the snow. That one already worked out. Remove *flies* from hat. Flies so easily droppable. Memorise a check list. Above all, keep calm. He wouldn't even look after the boulder, to see what happened. There couldn't be any doubt, after all. And no one else would be looking. Brucie wouldn't. *That* was the vital element: still the one that needed working on. But before they reached the distillery he'd worked that one out, too.

The Glentorran was a small family pot-still whose raw product was in high demand for premium blends. Rarely, bottles of the mature single malt appeared in the haunts of butlers at the highest of Highland Flings. More rarely still, a sacred bottle of Partners' Reserve became available every millenium or so, for royalty and above. None of the Reserve was below forty years old, its padlocked oak casks under religious scrutiny by the Excise authorities. However there was a mysterious evaporation known as ullage . . . Brucie was still holding forth on this mystery as they entered the ramshackle gates.

Brucie had friends at the Glentorran and they were soon having tiny samples as they made the rounds. At Waring's behest Brucie discreetly inquired into ullage, and before they left a lorry driver was asking him as a special favour to deliver a small wee food parcel to an old auntie

26

of his, now very infirm; and fifteen pounds of Waring's money had changed hands.

Waring took charge of the food parcel himself as they returned after lunch. There was barely half a pint in it, and it had not ulled from the oldest of the casks; but its antiquity still seemed to have Brucie in a trance.

'Should we no' just *try* a drop?' he asked.

'Tomorrow. At elevenses,' Waring said. 'As a final celebration. If I've caught anything to celebrate.'

He thought he would be needing a drop by then. He thought they all would; except one, of course.

And that sewed Brucie up. D·Day ahead.

D·Day dawned dim, but afterwards turned absolutely marvellous: the perfection prophesied by Brucie. The wind had dropped, the snow was hard, the sky was blue and a sun of exceptional cheeriness shone in it. Waring suspected all this. There was too much general goodness about. He saw he would need more and not less determination in such blithe conditions, and concentrated grimly on his check list.

Brucie met them with a face so unnaturally ravaged by smiles as to be almost unrecognisable. 'Mr and Mrs Waring, Mr Clintock! Did I deliver the right weather?'

'You did, Brucie, you did,' Nigel said genially.

'A fine bonny fish for you today, Mr Waring!'

'I hope so,' Waring said.

'For sure, for sure. Have we got everything? Your wee bit rope,' he said, nodding with great good humour at Waring's coil. 'Everything *else*?' His eyes were roaming.

Estelle patted her bag. 'All here, Brucie.'

'Ah, we'll have a grand morning!'

He got them in the car, and out of it, and bustled about the hut with such pleasing deference that it wasn't till he was striding ahead of them with the tackle to the

Blackrock that Waring noticed Estelle was without her bag.

'He'll drive me round the bend this morning,' she said, vexed. 'It must be in the car. We can get it later.'

'He won't forget. His mind is wonderfully concentrated today.'

He kept his own mind that way.

'Brucie,' he said as they were on the river bank, 'a word in your ear. I want to catch something today.'

'You will, you will, Mr Waring. Make no doubt!'

'I'll try the fly, but I'd like to give the spinner a go, too.'

'Where's the harm in it?' said Brucie tolerantly.

'And I'll cover as much water as possible. So keep an eye on me, and when I give the word just run every bit of tackle I'm not using down to the next pool.'

'Good as done,' Brucie said. 'I'll be up yonder, watching the pair of you, you and Mr Clintock both.'

'I'll give you a wave. I'll blow the whistle. Just come right down and get the stuff and I'll follow you round.'

'Rely on me.'

'And if I'm lucky – a *special* celebration, remember.'

'Say no more, Mr Waring,' said Brucie, chuckling. 'If you're all set I'll just take a wee look at Mr Clintock, get him off right.'

'But watch out for me, mind.'

'I will, sir. Be of good heart.'

Waring's heart wasn't good. It was bumping unevenly. He couldn't believe he'd be doing it within the hour; in less than *half* an hour. It was gone half past nine now. Nigel would be in position in thirty minutes. It was happening too fast. And in conditions he hadn't expected. He'd imagined a harsh scene of wind and snow, himself doggedly going about the task, almost a part of the natural violence, a part he might later confuse, even forget. In this smiling day none of it seemed real.

28

He slipped the bight of rope over his head.

'Henry, do be careful. It's still very fast.'

'I'll be all right.'

'Don't go so far.'

He didn't answer her. He tightened the rope, took his fly rod and gaff and went out along the spit. He entered the water carefully, knowing about it now, using the gaff cannily. The force of it still almost knocked him sideways, but he braced himself and proceeded. Keep careful check of the time. He'd get in position and try a few casts. He'd have to do that.

He found the position, the boulder he'd found before, and steadied himself at it again. Everything seemed absurdly unreal; the uproar, the tumultuous water, his own physical danger in it, apart from the coming dangers. But he did not feel danger. Unreal, all of it. He thought perhaps he had to feel like this, that he'd subconsciously prepared himself for it. Some part of him was going on working. He was stripping off line. He was swishing the big rod there and back. He had his line out fishing. And it was part of the unreality that almost at once he was into a fish. He felt it, with his finger; felt it without any question. The unseen salmon took the fly, turned, checked. He let it go, didn't strike, felt the fly run free again. The powerful beast would take upwards of twenty minutes to play, to tire out, and then would have to be beached. He didn't have twenty minutes.

He looked at his watch and saw that he had fifteen: it was twenty to ten. Before ten to, he would turn and give Brucie the signal in his hut. At five to, he would check that Brucie was down on the beach and going off with the tackle: going off in the other direction. He could start moving then.

He cast half a dozen times more, all from the same position. He knew Brucie, if watching, wouldn't approve. You had to move steadily down the beat. He wasn't moving from where he was, not till necessary.

Before ten to, he halted and closed his eyes in the torrent and went over the check list. Then he opened them and checked the whistle. He did it balancing awkwardly, with the hand holding the gaff, and right away the whistle came off its lanyard. First damned thing. *After use, lose whistle.* He didn't want to lose it elsewhere. It unsettled him suddenly and a touch of vertigo came on. He closed his eyes again and put it out of mind; and with eyes still closed stripped off some line. He had to be seen to be in action. He opened his eyes and cast, and again as if in a dream was immediately into a fish.

He knew then it was going to be all right. There was an inevitable feeling about it. It was the feeling he'd had in hospital: something that seemed totally incredible was in fact happening.

He let the fish go, and checked with his watch, and got the whistle in his teeth, and turned and blew. He waved at the same time, and saw a tiny answering movement out-side the hut, and with the strangest feeling knew that it was now on. It was on! He got the line out a couple of times more, not even watching it, and turned, and saw Brucie was picking up the tackle and walking away.

He was walking the wrong way.

He was walking towards Nigel.

Waring blinked, and shook his head to clear it, and looked again. Brucie was still walking the wrong way.

He blew the whistle. He blew as hard as he could, and waved, and saw Brucie turn and motion to him. But he still kept walking in the same direction and didn't look back any more.

Something had gone terribly wrong; Waring knew it. He blew and kept blowing, but Brucie didn't turn and he saw that he couldn't hear him.

Brucie heard quite well, and clucked to himself. The wee man could surely wait a few minutes. The missus had just this minute told him she'd left her bag with the Reserve in the car and would he take it in preparation to the hut. For sure he would! He'd have a quick wee glance to see how Clintock was doing below at the same time – tips due from both of them – and get the Reserve and pop it in the hut and from there run directly with the tackle down to the other pool. He had the tackle with him now. In a question of something like the Reserve did a few minutes here and there matter? The wee man was keeping on with his whistle, tooting away. It seemed more discreet just to keep on and no' look back. So Brucie didn't.

Waring spat the whistle out and started for the bank. There were still minutes in hand and he could still turn him around. He waved wildly at Estelle, and she responded at once. He felt the tension come on the rope.

It came too hard. She was pulling like mad. He signalled her not to pull so hard, but she kept on, and he clutched tightly on the rope, leaning back on it. He had to clutch so tightly, the rod slipped from his hand, and he let it go. He had the line still out, and it caught in some way about his ears, and then his neck. With the same sense of unreality he suddenly realised that he was into another fish. Or rather, the fish was into him. The fish had the fly. He did not have the rod.

At just about the moment that he realised this, Waring realised something else. Estelle had let go of the rope.

He was leaning heavily against its pull, and then there was no pull, and he was on his back, in the torrent.

He felt the icy water pouring into the top of his waders, and tried to stand, and couldn't. He was waterlogged. He was also in some way going backwards, at speed. He was no longer in control. Something else was in control. For fleeting moments he got his arms out and waved. He saw

Estelle was waving back, and mouthing something. He couldn't hear her, but he saw she was smiling.

In a series of simultaneous impressions he registered a number of things. He registered a grating feeling under his back. He registered that Nigel was wrong and Estelle didn't want to hang on to him, for she had let him go. She had let all the rope go. He realised that the grating under his back was caused by the ridge of rock that formed the wall of the pool, and that the salmon had just taken him into the pool. And he realised finally – with a kind of rage that he had not experienced when seeing it all go before – what it was that Estelle was mouthing as she continued to smile so. It was only one word, but she kept on mouthing it. And her hand kept waving goodbye too.

Colin Dexter

AT THE LULU-BAR MOTEL

I shall never be able to forget what Louis said – chiefly, no doubt, because he said it so often, a cynical smile slowly softening that calculating old mouth of his: 'People are so gullible!' –that's what he kept on saying, our Louis. And I've used those self-same words a thousand times myself – used them again last night to this fat-walleted coach-load of mine as they debussed at the Lulu-Bar Motel before tucking their starched napkins over their legs and starting into one of Louis' five-star four-coursers, with all the wines and a final slim liqueur. Yes, people are so gullible . . . Not *quite* all of them (make no mistake!) – and please don't misunderstand me. This particular manifestation of our human frailty is of only marginal concern to me personally, since occasionally I cut a thinnish slice of that great cake for myself – as I did just before I unloaded those matching sets of leather cases and hulked them round the motel corridors.

But let's get the chronology correct. All that hulking around comes right after we've pulled into the motel where – as always – I turn to all the good people (the black briefcase tight under my right arm) and tell them we're here, folks; here for the first-night stop on a wunnerful tour, which every single one o' you is goin' to enjoy real great. From tomorrow – and I'm real sorry about this, folks – you won't have me personally lookin' after you any more; but that's how the operation operates. I'm just the first-leg man myself, and someone else'll have the real privilege of drivin' you out on the second leg post-breakfast. Tonight itself, though, I'll be hangin' around the cocktail bar (got that?), and if you've any problems about – well, about *anything,* you just come along and talk to me, and we'll sort things out real easy. One thing, folks. Just one small friendly word o' counsel to you all. There's one or two guys around these parts who are about as quick an' as slick an' as smooth as a well-soaped ferret. Now, the last thing I'd ever try to do is stop you enjoyin' your vaycay-tions, and maybe one or two of you could fancy your chances with a deck o' cards against the deadliest dealer from here to Detroit. But... well, as I say, just a friendly word o' counsel, folks. Which is this: *some people are so gullible!* – and I just wouldn't like it if any o' you – well, as I say, I just wouldn't like it.

That's the way I usually dress it up, and not a bad little dressing up, at that, as I think you'll agree. 'O.K.' (do I hear you say?) 'If some of them want to transfer their savings to someone else's account – so what? You can't live other folks' lives for them, now can you? You did your best, Danny boy. So forget it!' Which all makes good logical sense, as I know. But they still worry me a little – all those warm-hearted, clean-living folk, because – well, simply because they're so gullible. And if you don't relish reading about such pleasant folk who plop like juicy pears into the pockets of sharp-fingered charlatans – well, you're not going to like this story. You're not going to like it one little bit.

Most of them were in their sixties or early seventies (no children on the Luxi-Coach Package Tours), and as they filed past the old driving cushion they slipped me a few bucks each and thanked me for a real nice way to start a vaycaytion. After that it took a couple of hours to hump all that baggage around the rooms, and it was half-past eight

34

before I got down to some of Lucy's chicken curry. Lucy? She's a honey of a girl – the sort of big-breasted blonde that most of my fellow sinners would willingly seek to seduce and, to be honest with you – But let me return to the theme.

The cocktail bar is a flashily furnished, polychrome affair, with deep, full-patterned carpet, orange imitation-leather seats and soft wall-lighting in a low, pink glow; and by about half-past nine the place was beginning to fill up nicely. Quite a few of them I recognized from the coach: but there were others. Oh yes, there were a few others . . .

He wasn't a big fellow – five–six, five–seven – and he wore a loud check suit just like they used to do on the movies. When I walked in he was standing by the bar, a deck of cards shuttling magically from hand to hand. 'Fancy a game, folks? Lukey's the name.' He was pleasant enough, I suppose, in an ugly sort of way; and with his white teeth glinting in a broad-mouthed smile, you could almost stop disliking him. Sometimes.

It was just before ten when he got his first bite – a stocky, middle-aged fellow who looked as if he could take pretty good care of himself, thank you. So. So, I watched them idly as they sat opposite each other at one of the smooth-topped central tables, and it wasn't long before a few others began watching, too. It was a bit of interest – a bit of an incident. And it wasn't *their* money at stake.

Now Lukey loved one game above all others, and I'll have to bare its bones a bit if you're going to follow the story. (Be patient, please: we're running along quite nicely now.) First, it's a dollar stake in the kitty, all right? Then two cards are dealt to each of the players, the court cards counting ten, the ace eleven, and all the other cards living up to their marked face-value. Thus it follows, as day follows night and as luck follows Luke, that the gods are grinning at you if you pick up a ten and an ace – for that is vingt-et-un, my friends, whether you reckon by fahrenheit or centigrade, and twenty-one's the best they come. And so long as you remember not to break that twenty-one mile speed-limit, you can buy as many more cards as you like and – But I don't think you're going to have much trouble in following things.

It was the speed with which hand followed hand that surprised all the on-lookers, since our challenger ('Call me Bart') was clearly no stranger to the Lukesberry rules and five or six hands were through every minute. Slap! A dollar bill in the kitty. Slap! A dollar bill on top. Flick, flick; flick, flick; buy; stick; bust. Dollar, dollar; flick, flick; quicker ever quicker. Soon I'm standing behind Bartey and I can see his cards. He picks up a ten, and a four; and without mulling it over for a micro-second he says 'Stick'. Then Lukey turns over a seven, and an eight – and then he flicks over another card for himself – a Jack. Over the top! And Bartey pockets yet another kitty; and it's back to that dollar-dollar, flick-flicking again. And when Bart wins again, Luke asks him nicely if he'd like to deal. But Bart declines the kind offer. 'No,' he says. 'I'm on a nice li'l winnin' streak here, pal, so just you keep on dealing them pretty li'l beauties same as before – that's all I ask.'

So Lukey goes on doing just that; and by all that's super-sonic what a sharp our Lukey is! I reckon you'd need more than a slow-motion replay to appreciate that prestissimo prestidigitation of his. You could watch those fingers with the eagle eye of old Cortes – and yet whether he was flicking the cards from the top or the middle or the bottom, I swear no one could ever tell. In spite of all this, though, Bartey-boy is still advancing his winnings. Now he picks up a seven, and a four; and he decides to buy another card for ten dollars. So Lukey covers the ten dollars from his fat roll, deals Bartey a nine – and things are looking mighty good. Then Luke turns over his own pair (why he bothers, I can't really say, for he knows them all along): a six, and a nine, they are – and things look pretty bad. He turns over another card from the deck – an eight. And once more he's out of his dug-out and over the top.

'My luck'll change soon,' says Luke.

'Not with me, it won't,' says Bart, picking up the twenty-two dollars from the kitty.

'You quitting, you mean?'

'I'm quitting,' says Bart.

'You've played before, I reckon.'

'Yep.'

'You always quit when you're winning?'

'Yep.'

Luke says nothing for a few seconds. He just picks up the deck and looks at it sourly, as if something somewhere in the universe has gone mildly askew. Then he calls on the power of the poets and he quotes the only lines he's ever learned:

'Bartey,' he says,

' "If you can make one heap of all your winnings
    And risk it on one turn of pitch and toss . . ."

Remember that? What about it? You've taken seventy odd dollars off o' me, and I'm just suggestin' that if you put 'em in the middle – and if I cover 'em . . . What do you say? One hand, that's all.'

The audience was about thirty strong now, and as many were urging Bartey on as were urging him off. And they were all pretty committed, too – one way or the other. One of them in particular . . .

I'd seen him earlier at the bar, and a quaint little fellow he was, too. By the look of him he was in his mid- or late-seventies, no more than four-ten, four-eleven, in his built-up shoes. His face was deeply tanned and just as deeply lined, and he wore a blazer gaudily striped in red and royal blue. Underneath the blazer pocket, tastelessly yet lovingly picked out in purple cotton, was the legend: Virgil K. Perkins Jnr. Which made you wonder whether Virgil K. Perkins Snr. was still somewhere in circulation – although a further glance at his senile son seemed to settle that particular question in the negative. Well, it's this old-timer who tries pretty hard to get Bartey to pocket his dollars and call it a night. And for a little while it seemed that Bartey was going to listen. But no. He's tempted – and he falls.

'Okey doke,' says Bartey. 'One more hand it is.'

It was Luke now who seemed to look mildly uneasy as he covered the seventy-odd dollars and squared up the deck. From other parts of the room the crowd was rolling up in force again: forty, fifty of them now, watching in silence as Luke dealt the cards. Bartey let his pair of cards lie on the table a few seconds and his hands seemed half full of the shakes as he picked them up. A ten; and a six. Sixteen. And for the first time that evening he hesitated, as he fell to figuring out the odds. Then he said 'Stick'; but it took him twice to say it because the first "stick" got sort of stuck in his larynx. So it was Lukey's turn now, and he slowly turned over a six – and then a nine. Fifteen. And Luke frowned a long time at his fifteen and his right hand toyed with the next card on the top of the deck, quarter turning it, half turning it, almost turning it – and then putting it back.

'Fifteen,' he said.

'*Sixteen*,' says Bartey, and his voice was vibrant as he grabbed the pile of notes in the middle.

Then he was gone.

The on-lookers were beginning to drift away as Luke sat still in his seat, the cards still shuttling endlessly from one large palm to the other. It was the old boy who spoke to him first.

'You deserve a drink, sir!' he says. 'Virgil K. Perkins Junior's the name, and this is my li'l wife, Minny.'

'We're from Omaha,' says Minny dutifully.

And so Virgil gets Luke a rye whisky, and they start talking.

'You a card player yourself, Mr Perkins?'

'Me? No, sir,' says Virgil. 'Me and the li'l wife here' (Minny was four or five inches the taller) 'were just startin' on a vaycaytion together, sir. We're from Omaha, just like she says.'

But the provenance of these proud citizens seemed of no great importance to Luke. 'A few quick hands, Mr Perkins?'

'No,' says Virgil, with a quiet smile.

'Look, Mr Perkins! I don't care − I just don't *care* − whether it's winnin' or losin', and that's the truth. Now if we just −'

'No!' says Virgil.

'You musta heard of beginner's luck?'

'*No!*' says Virgil.

'You're from Omaha, then?' says Luke, turning all pleasant-like to Minny . . .

I left them there, walked over to the bar, and bought an orange juice from Lucy, who sometimes comes through to serve about ten o'clock. She's wearing a lowly cut blouse, and a highly cute hair-style. But she says nothing to me; just winks − unsmilingly.

Sure enough, when I returned to the table, there was Virgil K. Perkins "just tryin' a few hands", as he put it; and I don't really need to drag you through all the details, do I? It's all going to end up exactly as you expect . . . but perhaps I'd better put it down, if only for the record; and I'll make it all as brief as I can.

From the start it followed the usual pattern: a dollar up;

a dollar down. Nice and easy, take it gently; and soon the little fellow was beaming broadly, and picking up his cards with accelerating eagerness. But, of course, the balance was slowly swinging against him: twenty dollars down; thirty; forty . . .

'Lucky little run for me,' says Luke with a disarming smile, as if for two dimes he'd shovel all his winnings across the table and ease that ever-tightening look round Virgil's mouth. It was all getting just a little obvious, too, and surely someone soon would notice those nimble fingers that forever flicked those eights and nines when only fours and fives could save old Virgil's day. And someone did.

'Why don't you let the old fella deal once in a while?' asks one.

'Yeah, why not?' asks another.

'You wanna deal, pop?' concedes Luke.

But Virgil shakes his white head. 'I've had enough,' he says. 'I shouldn't really –'

'Come on,' says Minny gently.

'He can deal. Sure he can, if he wants to,' says Luke.

'He can't deal off the bottom, though!'

Luke was on his feet in a flash, looking round the room. 'Who said that?' he asked, and his voice was tight and mean. All conversation had stopped, and no one was prepared to own up. Least of all me – who'd said it.

'Well,' said Luke, as he resumed his seat, 'that does it, pop! If I'm bein' accused of cheatin' by some lily-livered coward who won't repeat such villainous vilification – then we'll have to settle the question as a matter of honour, I reckon. *You* deal, pop!'

The old man hesitated – but not for too long. "Honour" was one of those big words with a capital letter, and wasn't a thing you could shove around too lightly. So he picked up the cards and he shuffled them, boxing and botching the whole business with an awkwardness almost unmatched in the annals of card-play. But somehow he managed to square the deck – and he dealt.

'I'll buy one,' says Luke, slipping a ten-dollar bill into the middle.

Virgil slowly covers the stake, and then pushes over a card.

'Stick,' says Luke.

Taking from his blazer pocket an inordinately large handkerchief, the old man mops his brow and turns his own cards over: a queen; and – an ace!

Luke merely shrugs his shoulders and pushes the kitty across: 'That's the way to do it, pop! Just you keep dealing yourself a few hands like that and –'

'No!' cries Minny, who'd been bleating her forebodings intermittently from the very beginning.

But Virgil lays a gentle hand on her shoulder: 'Don't be cross with me, old girl. And don't *worry!* I'm just a-goin' to deal myself one more li'l hand and . . .'

And another, and another, and another. And the gods were not smiling on the little man from Omaha: not the slightest sign of the meanest grin. Was it merely a matter of saving Face? Of preserving Honour? No, sir! It seemed just plain desperation as the old boy chased his losses round and round that smooth-topped table, with Minny sitting there beside him, her eyes tightly closed as if she was pinning the remnants of her hopes in the power of silent prayer. (I hitched the briefcase tighter under my right arm as I caught sight of Lucy behind the crowd, her eyes holding mine – again unsmilingly.)

By half-past ten Virgil K. Perkins Jnr. had lost one thousand dollars, and he sat there crumpled up inside his chair. It wasn't as if he was short of friends, for the large audience had been behind him all along, just willing the old fellow to win. And it wasn't as if anyone could blame

41

our nimble-fingered Lukey any more, for it was Virgil himself who had long since been dealing out his own disasters.

Not any longer, though. He pushed the deck slowly across the table and stood up. 'I'm sorry, old girl,' he says to Minny, and his voice is all choked up. 'It was your money as much as mine –'

But Luke was leaning across and he put his mighty palm on the old boy's skinny wrist. And he speaks quietly. 'Look, pop! You've just lost yourself a thousand bucks, right? So I want you to listen to me carefully because I'm gonna tell you how we can put all that to rights again. Now, we'll just have one more hand –'

'NO!' (The little old lady's voice was loud and shrill this time.) 'He *won't!* He won't lay down another dollar, d'you hear me? He's just – he's just a poor old fool, can't you see that? He's just a gullible, poor old –' But the rest of her words were strangled in her throat, and Virgil sat down again and put his arm round her shoulder as she began to weep silently.

'Don't you *want* to get all your money back?' Luke's voice is quiet again, but everyone can hear his words.

'Don't listen to him!' shouts one.

'Call it a day, sir!' shouts another.

Says Luke, turning to all of them: 'Old pop, here, he's got one helluva sight more spunk in him than the rest o' you put together! And, what's more, not a single man jack o' you knows the proposition I'm proposin'. Well?' (Luke looks around real bold.) 'Well? *Do* you?'

It was all silence again now, as Luke looks across to Virgil and formulates his offer. 'Look, pop. I've been mighty lucky tonight, as I think you might agree. So, I'm going to give you the sort o' chance you'll never have again. And this is what we'll do. We'll have just one last hand and we'll take two points off my score. Got that? I

42

pick up eighteen – we call it sixteen. And just the same whatever score it is. What do you say, pop?'

But old Virgil – he shakes his head. 'You're a good sport, Luke, but –'

'Let's make it *three* off then,' says Luke earnestly. 'I pick up twenty – we call it seventeen. O.K? Look, pop!' (He leans across and grips the wrist again.) 'Nobody's *ever* gonna make you any better offer than that. *Nobody.* You know something? It's virtually *certain* you're gonna get all that lovely money right back into that wallet o' yours, now, isn't it?'

It was tempting. Ye gods, it was tempting! And it was soon clear that the audience was thinking it was pretty tempting, too, with a good many of them revising their former estimate of things.

'What d'you say?' asks Luke.

'No,' says Virgil. 'It's not just me – it's Minny here. I've made enough of a fool of myself for one night, haven't I, old girl?'

Then Minny looked at him, straight on, like. A surprising change had come over her tear-stained face, and her blue eyes blazed with a sudden surge of almost joyous challenge, 'You take him on, Virgil!' she says, with a quiet, proud authority.

But Virgil still sat there dejected and indecisive. His hands ran across that shock of waving white hair, and for a minute or two he pondered to himself. Then he decided. He took most of the remaining notes from his wallet, and counted them with lingering affection before stacking them neatly in the centre of the table. 'Do you wanna count 'em, Luke?' he says. And it was as if the tide had suddenly turned; as if the old man sensed the smell of victory in his nostrils.

For a few seconds now it seemed to be Luke who was nervy and hesitant, the brashness momentarily draining

43

from him. But the offer had been taken up, and the fifty or sixty onlookers were in no mood to let him forget it. He slowly counted out his own bills, and placed them on the top of Virgil's.

Two thousand dollars – on one hand.

Luke has already picked up the deck, and now he's shuffling the spots with his usual, casual expertise.

'Why are *you* dealin'?'

Luke looks up, and stares me hard in the eye. 'Was that *you* just spoke, mister?'

I nod. 'Yep. It was me. And I wanna know why it is you think you got some goddam right to deal them cards – because you don't deal 'em straight, brother. You flick 'em off the top and you flick 'em off the bottom and for all I know you flick em –'

'I'll see you outside, mister, as soon as –'

'You'll do no such thing,' I replies quietly. 'I just ain't goin' to be outside no more tonight again – least of all for you, brother.'

He looked mighty dangerous then – but I just didn't care. The skin along his knuckles was growing white as he slowly got to his feet and moved his chair backwards. And then, just as slowly, he sat himself down again – and he surprises everybody. He pushes the deck over the table and he says: 'He's right, pop. *You* deal!'

Somehow old pop's shaking hands managed to shuffle the cards into some sort of shape; and when a couple of cards fall to the floor, it's me who bends down and hands them back to him.

'Cut,' says pop.

So Luke cuts – about half way down the deck (though knowing Lukey I should think it was *exactly* half way down). Miraculously, it seems, old Virgil's hands had gotten themselves rid of any shakes, and he deals the cards out firm and fine: one for Luke, one for himself;

44

another for Luke, and another for himself. For a few moments each man left them lying there on the top of the table. Then Luke picks up his own – first the one, and then the other.

'Stick!' he says, and his voice is a bit hoarse.

Every eye in the room was now on Virgil as he turned over his first card – a seven; then the second card – a ten. Seventeen! And all you've got to do, my friends, is to add on three – and that's a handsome little twenty, and the whole room was mumbling and murmuring in approval.

Every eye now switches to Luke, and in the sudden tense silence the cards are slowly turned: first a king, and then – ye gods! – an ace! And as Lukey smiles down at that beautiful twenty-oner the audience groaned like they always do when its favourite show-jumper knocks the top off the last fence.

And where, my friends, do we go from there? Well, I'll tell you. It was Lucy who started it all immediately Luke had left. She pushed her way through the on-lookers and plunged her hand deep down between those glorious breasts of hers to clutch her evening's tips.

'Mr Perkins, isn't it? I know it isn't all that much; but – but if it'll help, please take it.' About seven or eight dollars, it was, no more – but, believe me, it bore its fruit two-hundred-fold. It was me who was next. I'd taken about thirty-five dollars on the coach and (once more hitching the old briefcase higher under my arm) I fished it all out of my back pocket and placed it a-top of Lucy's crumpled offerings.

'Mr Perkins,' I said sombrely. 'You should've been on *my* coach, old friend.' That's all I said.

As for Virgil, he said nothing. He just sat back all crumpled up like before, with Minny sobbing silently beside him. I reckon he looked as if he couldn't trust himself to say a single word. But it didn't matter. All the audience was sad and sullenly sympathetic – and, as I said, they'd had their fill of Louis' vintage wines. And I've got to hand it to them. Twenty dollars; another twenty dollars; a fifty; a few tens; another twenty; another fifty – I watched them all as these clean-living, God fearing folk forked something from their careful savings. And I reckon there wasn't a single man-jack of them who didn't make his mark upon that ever-mounting pile. But still Virgil said nothing. When finally he stumbled his way to the exit, holding Minny in one hand and a very fat pile of other people's dollars in the other, he turned round as if he was going to say something to all his very good friends. But still the words wouldn't come, it seemed; and he turned once more and left the cocktail bar.

I woke late the next morning, and only then because Luke was leaning over me, gently shaking me by the shoulder.

'Louis says he wants to see you at half-past ten.'

I lifted my left arm and focused on the wrist-watch: already five to ten.

'You all right, Danny?' Luke was standing by the door now (he must have had a key for that!) and for some reason he didn't look mightily happy.

'Sure, sure!'

'Half-past, then,' repeated Luke, and closed the door behind him.

I still felt very tired, and I was conscious that the back of my head was aching – and that's unusual for me. Nothing to drink the night before – well, only the odd orange juice that Lucy had . . . orange juice . . .? I fell to wondering slightly, and turned to look at the other side of the bed, where the sheet was neatly turned down in a white hypotenuse. Lucy had gone – doubtless gone early; but then Lucy was always sensible and careful about such things . . .

I saw my face frowning as I stood in front of the

shaving-mirror; and I was still frowning when I took the suit off the hanger in the wardrobe and noticed that the briefcase was gone. But I'd have been frowning even more if the briefcase *hadn't* gone; and as I dressed, my head was clearing nicely. I picked up the two thick sealed envelopes that had nestled all night under my pillow, put them, one each, into the pockets of my overcoat, and felt happy enough when I knocked on the door of Louis' private suite and walked straight in. It was ten thirty-two.

There were the usual six chairs round the oblong table, and four of them were taken already: there was Luke, and there was Barty; then there was Minny; and at the head of the table, Louis himself – a Louis still, doubtless, no more than four-ten, four-eleven in his built-up shoes, but minus that garishly striped blazer now; minus, too, that shock of silvery hair which the previous evening had covered that large, bald dome of his.

'You're late,' he says, but not unpleasantly. 'Sit down, Danny.' So I sat down, feeling like a little boy in the first grade. (But I usually feel like that with Louis.)

'You seen Lucy?' asks Minny, as Barty pours me a drop of Irish.

'Lucy? No – have you tried her room?'

But no one seemed much willing to answer that one, and we waited for a few minutes in silence before Louis spoke again.

'Danny,' he says, 'you'll remember that when we brought you into our latest li'l operation a few months back I figured we'd go for about a quarter of a million before we launched out on a new one?'

I nodded.

'Well, we're near enough there now as makes no odds – a fact perhaps you may yourself be not completely unaware of? After all, Danny, it was one o' your jobs to take my li'l Lucy down to the bank on Mondays, now

47

wasn't it? And I reckon you've got a pretty clear idea of how things are.'

I nodded again, and kept on looking him straight in the eyes.

'Well, it was never no secret from any of us – was it? – that I'd be transferrin' this li'l investment o' mine over to Luke and Bartholomew here as soon as they – well, as soon as they showed me they was worthy.'

I was nodding slowly all the time now; but he'd left something out. 'Lucy was goin' to be in it, too,' I said.

'You're very fond of my Lucy, aren't you?' says Minny quietly.

'Yep. I'm very fond of her, Minny.' And that was the truth.

'It's not bin difficult for any o' us to see that, old girl, now has it?' Louis turned to Minny and patted her affectionately on the arm. Then he focuses on me again. 'You needn't have no worries about my li'l daughter, Danny. No worries at all! Did it never occur to you to wonder just why I christened this latest li'l investment o' mine as the "Lulu-Bar Motel"?'

For a few seconds I must have looked a little puzzled, but my head was clearing nicely with the whisky, and I suddenly saw what he meant. Yes! What a deep old devil our Louis was! The *Lu*-cy, *Lu*-ke, *Bar*-tholomew Motel . . .

But Louis was still speaking: 'I only asked you down this mornin', Danny, because I was hopin' to wind it all up here and now – and to let you know how much I've bin aware o' your own li'l contribution. But – well, it's all tied up in a way with Lucy, isn't it? And I reckon' (he looked at Luke and Bart) 'I reckon we'd better call another li'l meeting tonight? About eight? All right?'

It seemed all right to all of us, and I got up to go.

'You off to town, Danny?' asks Louis, eyeing the overcoat.

'Yep.' That's all I said. Then I left them there and caught the bus to the station.

I'd always noticed it before: whenever I'd felt a bit guilty about anything it was as if I sensed that other people somehow seemed to *know*. But that's behind us now. And, anyway, it had been Lucy's idea originally – not mine. She'd needed me, of course, for devising the cheque and forging Louis' signature – for though I'm about as ham-fisted with a deck of cards as an arthritic octopus, I got my own particular specialism. Yes, sir! And Lucy trusted me, too, because I'd been carrying all that lovely money – 240,000 dollars of it! – all neatly stacked in five-hundred bills, all neatly enveloped and neatly sealed – why, I'd been carrying it all around with me in the old briefcase for two whole days! And Lucy – Lucy, my love! – we shall soon be meeting at the ticket-barrier on number one platform – and then be drifting off together quietly in the twilight . . .

At a quarter-to twelve I was there – standing in my overcoat and waiting happily. (Lucy had never been early in her life.) I lit another cigarette; then another. By twelve forty-five I was beginning to worry a little; by one forty-five I was beginning to worry a lot; and by two forty-five I was beginning to guess at the truth. Yet still I waited – waited and waited and waited. And, in a sense, I suppose, I've been waiting for Lucy ever since . . .

It was when the big hand on the station-clock came round to four that I finally called it a day and walked over to look at the Departure Board. I found a train that was due for New York in forty-five minutes, and I thought that that had better be that. I walked into the buffet and sat down with a coffee. So? So, here was yet another of life's illusions lying shattered in the dust, and yet . . . Poor, poor, lovely Lucy! I nearly allowed myself a saddened little smile as I thought of her opening up those two big envelopes in the briefcase – and finding there those 480 pieces of crisp, new paper, each exactly the size of a 500-dollar bill. She must have thought I was pretty – well, pretty gullible, I suppose, when we'd both agreed that *she* should take away the briefcase . . .

A single to New York would cost about fifty or sixty dollars, I reckoned; and as I joined what seemed to be the shorter queue at the ticket-office I took the bulky envelope from the right-hand pocket of the overcoat, opened it – and stood there stunned and gorgonized. Inside were about 240 pieces of crisp, new paper, each exactly the size of a 500-dollar bill; and my hands were trembling as I stood away from the queue and opened the other envelope. Exactly the same. Well, no – not *exactly* the same. On the top piece of blank paper there were three lines of writing in Louis' unmistakably minisculy hand:

I did my best to tell you Danny boy but you never did really understand that filosofy of mine now did you? It's just what I kept on telling you all along. People . . .

By now, though, I reckon you'll know those last few words that Louis wrote.

I walked back across to the buffet and ordered another coffee, counting up what I had in my pockets: just ten dollars and forty cents; and I fell to wondering where it was I went from here. Perhaps . . . perhaps there were one or two things in my favour. At least I could spell 'philosophy'; and then there was always the pretty big certainty (just as Louis said so often) that somewhere soon I'd find a few nice, kindly, gullible folk.

But as I glance around at the faces of my fellow men and women in the station buffet now, they all look very mean, and very hard.

Elizabeth Ferrars

INSTRUMENT OF JUSTICE

When Frances Liley read in the obituary column of *The Times* of the death of Oliver Darnell, beloved husband of Julia, suddenly at his home, she folded her arms on the table before her, put her head down on them and burst into violent tears. Anyone who had seen her then would have assumed that she was weeping at the loss of a dear friend. In fact, they were tears of relief, healing and wonderful. At last she was free. No threat hung over her any more. Or so she thought until she had had time to do a little thinking.

As soon as she had she sat back abruptly, dried her eyes roughly and sat staring before her, a dark, angularly hand-some woman of forty, possessed by a new horror. For when a person died his solicitor or his executors or someone would have to go through his papers and some-where they would find those terrible photographs. And God knew what would happen then. At least with Oliver, Frances had known where she was. Two thousand a year to him, which it had not been too difficult for her to find, and she had been relatively safe. But if someone else found the photographs and felt inclined to send them to Mark, her husband, he would immediately go ahead with the divorce that he wanted and would certainly get custody of their two children. That would be intolerable. She must think and think fast.

Luckily she had always had a quick brain. After only a few minutes she knew what to do, or at least what was worth trying. Telephoning Julia Darnell, she said, 'It's Frances, Julia. I've just seen the news about Oliver. I'm so terribly sorry. I can hardly believe it. It was his heart, was it? There was always something the matter with it, wasn't there? Listen, my dear, please be quite honest with me, but would you like me to come down? I mean, if you're alone now and I can help in any way. But don't say you'd like me to come if you'd sooner I didn't. Of course I'll come to the funeral, but I could come straight away and stay on for a few days, unless you've some other friend with you.'

Julia was tearfully grateful. She had no relations of her own and had never liked Oliver's, and though the neigh-bours, she said, had been very kind, she was virtually alone. And she and Frances were such very old friends, she could think of no one who could help so much to break the dreadful new loneliness of bereavement. Of course Julia had never known of her husband's brief adultery with Frances, or that he had supplemented his not very large income as a painter of very abstract pictures with a sideline in blackmail, and her affection for Frances was uncomplicated and sincere. Promising to arrive that afternoon, Frances telephoned Mark in his office to tell him what had happened and that she would probably be away for a few days. The children were no problem, because they were away at their boarding school. Packing a suitcase, she set off for the Darnells' cottage in Dorset.

By that time she had a plan of sorts in her mind. On the morning of the funeral she intended to wake up with what she would claim was a virus and say that she was feeling too ill to go out. Then, during the one time when she could be certain the cottage would be empty, she would make a swift search of it for the photographs. The

52

probability was that they were somewhere in Oliver's studio, a very private place in which Julia had never been allowed to touch anything, even to do a little cautious dusting. If they were not there, of course, if, for instance, Oliver had kept them in the bank, then there was nothing for Frances to do but go home and wait for the worst to happen, but with luck, she thought, she would find them.

Unfortunately her plan was wrecked by the fact that on the morning of the funeral it was Julia who woke up with a virus. She had a temperature of a hundred and two, complained of a sore throat and could only speak in a husky whisper. Frances called the doctor who gave Julia some antibiotics and said that she must certainly stay in bed and not go out into the chill of the February morning, even to attend her husband's funeral. Julia, with bright spots of fever on her plump, naturally pale cheeks, cried bitterly and said, 'But all those people coming back here to lunch, Frances — what *am* I to do about them? I can't possibly put them off now.'

For Julia had insisted that Oliver's relations, who were coming from a distance, and such neighbours as were kind enough to come to the funeral, must be given lunch in her house after it, and she and Frances had spent most of the day before assembling cold meats, salads, cheeses and a supply of rather inferior white wine for what Frances felt would be a gruesome little party, but the thought of which seemed to comfort Julia.

Again thinking fast, Frances said, 'Don't worry, I'll look after them for you. I'll go to the service, but I won't go on to the cemetery, I'll come straight back from the church and have everything ready for your friends when they arrive. Now just stay quiet and I'll look after everything.'

She gave Julia the pills that the doctor had left for her and also brought her a mug of hot milk into which she had emptied two capsules of sodium amytal which she had

53

found in the bathroom cabinet. They would almost certainly ensure that Julia would be asleep by the time that Frances returned from the church, and though she would not have as long for her search as she had hoped, she might still be fortunate.

There were not many people in the church. A man sitting next to Frances, who started a low-voiced conversation with her before the coffin had been brought in or the vicar appeared, introduced himself as Major Sowerby and said that his wife was desperately sorry not to be able to attend, but she was in bed with a virus.

'There's a terrible lot of it around in the village,' he said. 'Is it true poor Mrs Darnell's laid up with it too?'

'I'm afraid so,' Frances said.

'Tragic for her. Most upsetting. She and Oliver were so devoted to one another. Of course I didn't understand his painting, but Isobel, my wife, who knows a lot more about that sort of thing than I do, says he deserved much more recognition than he ever had. Great dedication, she says, and such integrity.'

'Oh, complete,' Frances agreed with a sweet, sad smile, and thought that in its way it was true. Oliver had been dedicated to exploiting any woman who had been fool enough to be charmed by his astonishing good looks and to trust him. As soon as the service was over she hurried out of the church, leaving the other mourners to go on to the cemetery, and made her way along the lane that led to the Darnells' cottage.

As she entered it, she stood still, listening. All was quiet. So it looked as if the sodium amytal had done its work and Julia was asleep. But just to make sure, Frances went to the foot of the stairs and called softly, 'Julia!'

There was no reply. She waited a moment, then wrenched off her coat, dropped it on a chair and went swiftly along the passage to Oliver's studio. Presently she would have to attend to the setting out of the lunch for Julia's guests, but the search must come first. Opening the door of the studio, she went in and only then understood the reason for the quiet in the house. Julia, in her dressing-gown, was lying in the middle of the floor with her head a terrible mass of blood and with a heavy hammer on the floor beside her.

Frances was not an entirely hard-hearted person. Also, she was by nature law-abiding. Her first impulse, as she stared at the battered thing on the floor, was to call the police. But then a habit that she had of having second thoughts asserted itself. It was still of desperate importance to her to find the photographs and once the police were in the house she would have no further chance of searching for them. That made the situation exceedingly complex. For one thing, how were the police to know that it had not been Frances whom Julia, drugged and half-asleep, had heard downstairs in her husband's studio, and coming downstairs to investigate, been killed by her for it? If Frances called the police now, she thought, she might find herself in deep trouble.

But if she did not and searched for the photographs first, she would presently find herself with a cooling body on her hands and sooner or later would have to explain why she had failed to report it a few hours earlier. It did not help that she was almost certain that she knew who the murderer was. A virus can be a very convenient thing, and Mrs Sowerby, who had not attended the church, would not have found out that Julia was ill and would have assumed that the house was empty. Looking round the studio, where drawers had been pulled out and papers, letters, sketches, notebooks, spilled on the floor, Frances wondered if the woman had found the photographs or letters that Oliver had presumably been holding over her before she committed murder, or if she was still in terror that someone else would find them. But even if she were, she was unlikely to come back for the present, knowing that a dozen guests would shortly be arriving. Taking the key out of the door, locking it on the outside and putting the key into the pocket of the suit that she was wearing, Frances went out to the kitchen to go on with preparing the lunch.

She took all the things that she and Julia had made the day before out of the refrigerator, spooned the various salads, the prawns with rice and peppers, the cucumbers in sour cream, the coleslaw and the rest, into cut glass bowls, arranged the slices of cold turkey, meat loaf and ham on dishes, and set them out on the table in the dining-room. She put silver and wine glasses on the table and drew the corks of several of the bottles of wine. The meal was only just ready when the first guests arrived.

They were the vicar, Arthur Craddock, and his wife. He was a slender, quiet-looking man whose voice, as he recited the psalms that Julia had chosen and described Oliver's improbable virtues, had seemed unexpectedly vibrant and authoritative. But any authority that he might achieve when he was performing his professional duties was sadly diminished, in a mere social setting, by his wife, a large, hearty woman who looked kindly, but accustomed to domination and who upset Frances at once by saying that she would just pop upstairs to have a few words with poor Julia, tell her how splendidly everything had gone off and how much she had been missed.

'But the infection,' Frances stammered. 'I believe it's all round the village and I know she wouldn't want you to be exposed to it here.'

'I'm never ill,' Mrs Craddock replied. 'Ask my husband. We were in India for a time, you know, and I've nursed patients through bubonic plague and never a whit the worse. I'm sure I could give Julia a little comfort.'

'Well, later, perhaps,' Frances said, recovering her presence of mind. 'I went up to see her myself a few minutes ago and found her asleep. The doctor gave her a sedative. He said rest was what she needed, and I'm sure he's right. I know she hasn't slept properly for days. But she's looking very peaceful now, so I don't think we should disturb her.'

'Ah no, of course not,' Mrs Craddock agreed. 'Was that Dr Bolling? Excellent man. The best type of good, old-fashioned family doctor whom you can really trust.'

She let herself and her husband be shepherded into the dining-room and they had each just accepted a glass of wine when the doorbell rang again and Frances left them to admit the next guests.

They were a brother and a cousin of Oliver's, both of whom, he had once told Frances, he knew disliked him. The next to arrive was Major Sowerby and gradually the dining-room filled, the hushed tones in which everyone spoke on first arriving rising by degrees until the noise in the room resembled that of any ordinary cocktail party. The food on the table was eaten with appetite, the wine was drunk, and the atmosphere became one of what seemed to Frances a faintly gruesome hilarity, quelled only now and again by guilt when someone was tactless enough to remind the others that these were funeral baked meats that they were consuming.

Slightly flushed, Oliver's brother remarked, 'Julia was always a jolly good cook. Pity she can't be with us now.'

'She must have taken a great deal of trouble over this,' Mrs Craddock said, 'but I expect it was good for her, taking her mind off her sorrow. I'd like to take a little of it up to her and tell her how we've all been thinking of her, because with all the noise we've been making I'm sure she must be awake by now. I'll just pop up with a plateful, shall I, and perhaps a glass of wine?'

'That's the ticket,' Major Sowerby said, 'though whisky might do her more good. I took a good strong whisky up to my wife before I left for the church, and a sandwich. She said a sandwich was all she could face. Actually I had to insist on her staying in bed, she was so upset at not being able to make it to the funeral, but obviously she wasn't fit to go out. The fact is, you know, she thought a lot of Oliver. Sat for her portrait to him once, then made me buy the thing. Well, I didn't mind doing it really, because no one could guess it's Isobel, it's all squares and triangles and she says it's good and she knows far more about that sort of thing than I do.'

Mrs Craddock was spooning prawns and rice on to a plate, murmuring, 'I wonder if she likes cucumber – it disagrees with some people,' adding a slice of turkey, a small piece of ham and reaching for a bottle of wine to fill a glass for Julia.

Frightened beyond words and desperate, Frances snatched the plate and the glass from the woman's hands, said brusquely, 'I'll take them,' made for the door and while Mrs Craddock was still only looking startled at her rudeness, shot up the stairs and through the open door into Julia's bedroom.

In its silence she first began to feel the real horror of the situation. Here she was with food and wine in her hands for a woman who lay in a room downstairs with her body cooling and her head battered in. Her gaze held hypno-tized by the sight of the empty bed with its dented pillows and its blankets thrown back, Frances gulped down the wine, wishing that it was something stronger, then went downstairs again and put down the plate of untouched food on the dining-table.

'She drank the wine, but she wouldn't eat anything,' she said to Mrs Craddock. 'I gave her another of the pills the doctor left for her. She's very sleepy. I really think it's best to leave her alone.'

Frustrated in her desire to do good, the vicar's wife soon left, sweeping her husband along with her, and after that, one by one, the other guests departed. At last the house was empty and quiet again.

Too quiet, too desolate. The last hour had been the worst nightmare that Frances had ever lived through, but at least the crowd of chattering people had been a defence against thought. Now she could not escape from it any longer. There was the problem of the photographs and the problem of the corpse in the studio. Looking at the table littered with china, wine glasses and left-overs, she had an absurd idea that she might do the washing-up before trying to cope with the murder, but recognizing this for the idiocy that it was, and that her motive was only to put off doing what she must, she poured out a glass of whisky, sat down at the head of the table and tried to concentrate.

The photographs came first. She must nerve herself to go back into the studio and search for them. What she did next would depend to some extent on whether or not she found them. She could hardly bear to face the possibility that she might not. With the dreadful things in his hands, Mark would certainly be able to obtain custody of the children when he went ahead with the divorce that he wanted, and she would never submit to that. For apart from the pleasure that she took in the two dear girls, it would be intolerable to let Mark triumph over her.

She thought of the photographs, of which Oliver had only once allowed her a glimpse, of how appallingly revealing they were, and of the bitter amusement with which Mark would view them. They were, in their way, superb photographs. Oliver might not have been an out-standing painter, but as a photographer he had been highly skilled, as well as incredibly ingenious. She had had no suspicion of the presence of the camera in the room at the time when he had taken the pictures, and when he had told her how he had done it, she had almost had to laugh, it had been so clever. But now she must get them back. That was what she must do before she thought of anything else.

She went back into the studio. It was easier than she had thought that it would be to disregard Julia's body, the darkening blood and the murderous hammer. Locking the door in case anyone, that well-meaning busybody, Mrs Craddock, for instance, should think of coming back, she began on a methodical search of the drawers and cupboards. To her surprise, she found the photographs almost at once, not merely prints, but the negatives too, in a box in a cupboard which she thought had not yet been opened by the previous searcher.

She found several other photographs of a similar character. Feeling dizzy with relief, close to bursting into tears as she had when she had first read of Oliver's death, she studied these, which were of three women, and wondered which of them was of Isobel Sowerby. Frances knew nothing about her except that her husband did not think that she looked as if she consisted of squares and triangles. But none of the women did. They all had more curves than angles. And two of them looked rather young to be married to Major Sowerby, though that was not the sort of thing about which it was ever possible to be sure. Men of sixty sometimes married girls in their teens. However, Frances thought that Julia's murderess was probably the third woman, who was about her own age, big, heavy-breasted, rather plump, with a look of passion and violence about her. In fact, a formidable-looking woman, surely capable of murder. After studying her face for some minutes, Frances put her photographs, the prints and the negatives, back into the cupboard, took those of herself and the two younger women to the sitting-room, put them down on the hearth and set fire to them.

The negatives spat, blazed briefly and disappeared, making a pungent smell in the room. The prints curled at the edges and caught fire more slowly, but as she prodded them with the poker, they flared up, then smouldered into ash. Watching them, sitting on her heels, she waited until there was not a spark left, then stood up and went to the telephone.

She had a plan now, a plan of sorts. It was a gamble, but then what could she do that was not? Picking up the directory, she looked up the Sowerbys' number and dialled it.

To her satisfaction, it was a woman's voice that answered. Frances did not introduce herself.

'I've found what you were looking for,' she said softly.

There was a silence. Frances suddenly became aware of how her heart was thudding. For this was the moment when she would discover whether or not her gamble had paid off. She might have guessed totally wrongly. Mrs Sowerby might be an innocent woman who had been in bed all day with 'flu, feeling very ill, and if that were so, Frances would have to start thinking all over again. It seemed to her lunacy now that she had not called the police as soon as she had found Julia's body. If only she had known how simple it was going to be to find the photographs, she would have done so, and would have had plenty of time to destroy them before the police arrived. But there was not much point in thinking on those lines now. It was too late. She waited.

At last an almost whispering voice said in her ear, 'Who are you?'

She drew a shuddering breath. So she had been right. Her plan was working.

'A friend of Julia's,' she said. 'I think you'd better come here as soon as possible.'

'What do you want?' the voice asked.

'Your help,' Frances said.

'I can't come. I'm ill.'

'I think it would be advisable to make a quick recovery.'

'But I can't. My husband wouldn't hear of my going out.'

'That's your problem. I'll wait here for a little, but not for long.'

There was another silence, then the voice said, 'All right, I'll see what I can do.'

The telephone at the other end was put down. Frances put down the one that she was holding, realizing that the hand that had been gripping it was clammy with sweat and had left damp marks on the instrument. She wondered if that mattered, but decided that it did not. She would have another call to make presently, which would account for the fingerprints.

She waited an hour before there came a ring at the front door bell. The early dusk of the February afternoon was already dimming the daylight. She had spent some of the time while she had had to wait stripping Julia's body of the dressing-gown and night-dress that she was wearing and redressing it in pants and bra, jeans and sweater. It had been a terrible undertaking. In the middle of it she had felt faint and had had to go back to the sitting-room to give herself a chance to recover her self-control. But she had been afraid to wait until the other woman arrived and could help her in case the body stiffened too much to make the undressing of it possible. She knew nothing about how long it took for rigor mortis to set in. The blood-stained clothes that she removed were a problem and so was the hammer. She had not thought about that until after she had started undressing Julia, but in the end she made a bundle of them, took them out to the garage and put them into the boot of the Darnells' car. Then she went back into the house to wait.

When the ring at the door came at last and she went to answer it, she found the woman whom she had been expecting on the doorstep. Her guess about the photographs had been correct. Isobel Sowerby was a middle-aged woman, tall and thick-set, with thick dark hair to her shoulders, intense dark eyes and jutting lips. She was wearing slacks and a sheepskin jacket.

Staring at Frances with deep enmity, she said, 'What am I supposed to do now?'

'We're going to arrange a suicide,' Frances answered.

'I don't understand,' the other woman said. 'If you know so much, why haven't you turned me in?'

'Because I'm involved myself. I made the mistake of not calling the police as soon as I found the body. I wanted to find some photographs of me that Oliver had and I didn't think until it was too late how difficult it was going to be to explain how I'd managed not to find Julia as soon as I got back from the church. So I'm in almost as much trouble as you are. And I think the best thing for both of us to do is to put Julia into her car and send her over the cliffs into the sea. Suicide while the balance of her mind was disturbed by the death of her husband. I couldn't arrange it alone because she's too heavy for me to carry. I had to have help.'

'All right, whatever you say,' Isobel Sowerby said. 'But give me the photographs first.'

'Afterwards,' Frances said.

'No, now, or I won't help you.'

'Afterwards,' Frances repeated.

They looked at one another with wary antagonism, then Isobel Sowerby shrugged her shoulders.

'Let's get on with it then,' she said. 'I persuaded my husband to go to the golf club to get over the funeral, and he'll stay there for a time and have a few drinks, but he'll be home presently and it won't help us to have him asking me questions.'

'How did you get into the house this morning?' Frances asked. 'I've been wondering about that.'

'The back door was unlocked, as I knew it would be. We aren't particular about locking up round here.'

'And you left in a hurry when you heard me come in.'

'Yes. Now let's get on.'

It was almost dark by then and the garage doors could not be seen from the lane outside. There was no one to see them as they carried Julia's body from the house to the car, put it in the seat beside the driver's, covered it with a rug, got into the car themselves and with Isobel Sowerby driving, since she knew the roads, started towards the coast. She drove cautiously along the twisting lanes until at last they reached the cliff-top and saw the dark chasm of the sea ahead of them.

Stopping the car close to the edge of the cliff, she and Frances got out and between them moved Julia's body into the driving seat. After that it was only a case of turning on the engine again, putting the car into low gear, slamming the doors and standing back while it went slowly forward to the brink, seemed to teeter there for an instant, then went plunging down, the sound of the crash that it made as it hit the rocks below carrying up to them with a loudness which it seemed to Frances must carry for miles.

But afterwards there was no sign that anyone else had heard it. The darkness around them was silent. They started the long walk back.

They did not talk to one another as they walked and had reached the Darnells' cottage before Isobel Sowerby said, 'I don't know what I'm going to say to my husband. He'll have got back from the golf club long ago.'

'You'll think of something,' Frances said. She did not think that Major Sowerby would be difficult to delude.

'You could always say you've been wandering around in a state of delirium.'

'Which is what I think I've been doing,' Isobel Sowerby said. 'Now give me the photographs.'

Frances took her into the sitting-room and showed her the heap of ashes in the gate.

'I burnt them.'

Isobel Sowerby stared at them incredulously, then broke suddenly into hysterical laughter.

'What a fool I am!' she cried. 'I've always been a fool. I needn't have come at all!'

'But I needed your help, so naturally I wasn't going to tell you that,' Frances replied.

'Are those really my photographs? You really destroyed them?'

'Along with some of my own. I'd get home now as soon as I could if I were you, because I'm going to telephone the police and tell them Julia's missing.'

Still laughing, Isobel Sowerby turned and plunged out into the darkness.

Frances went to the telephone, called the police and told them that she was very concerned because she had just discovered that Mrs Darnell, who was suffering from a high fever and was in a state of shock after the death of her husband, had disappeared. Her car was missing too. Frances said that she had only just discovered this, because after the lunch that had been held in the house after the funeral, she had felt so tired that she had gone to her room to lie down and had fallen asleep and had only just woken up, gone into Mrs Darnell's room to see how she was and found it empty. She said that she knew that Mrs Darnell had been in her room at about half past one, when she had taken some food and wine up to her and Mrs Darnell had drunk a little wine but had refused the food. But at what time she had got up and gone out Frances had no idea, because she had been so sound asleep. She had heard nothing. Anything might have happened in the house without her being aware of it.

The man who answered her call said that someone would be out to see her shortly. Putting the telephone down, Frances fetched a dustpan and brush, swept up the ashes in the grate and flushed them down the lavatory. Then in truth feeling as tired as she had told the police-man that she had felt earlier, she began to clear up the dining-room and had started on the washing-up when the police arrived.

After that everything went surprisingly smoothly. The police soon found the wreck of the car on the rocks at the foot of the cliffs and the hammer and the blood-stained nightdress and dressing-gown in the boot. They also found fingerprints on the steering-wheel which were later identi-fied as Mrs Sowerby's and they found some highly obscene photographs of her in a cupboard in Oliver Darnell's studio. It had happened too that Major Sowerby, in a state of great anxiety at finding his wife missing when he returned from the golf club, had telephoned several friends to ask if she was with them, so without his intend-ing it, he had destroyed any chance that she might have had of concocting an alibi. She told an absurd story about having been summoned by Mrs Liley to help her get rid of the body of Julia Darnell, whom she and not Isobel Sowerby had murdered, but the story was not believed. There was a little doubt as to whether she could have handled the body by herself, but she was a big, powerful woman and it was thought that she could and she was charged with the murder. Frances stayed on in the Darnells' cottage until after the inquest, then when her presence was no longer required, telephoned Mark and started for home.

As she drove, she fell into one of her rare moods of self-examination. She was not a nice person, she thought. Some people might even say of her that she was rather horrible. She did not really blame Mark for wanting to leave her and marry that little pudding of a woman who had been infatuated with him for the last five years. And if only he would give up his claim to the children, Frances would be quite willing to let him go. But they were the only people for whom she had ever felt any deep and lasting love. Or what she took to be love. It did not involve questioning whether it would be better for them to stay with her or with Mark, or which of their parents the girls themselves loved most. Even in her present mood of introspection, she did not ask herself that. She simply knew that they were hers, a possession from which it would be intolerable to be parted.

And horrible as perhaps she was, was she not an instrument of justice? Had she not arranged the arrest of Julia's murderess, without herself or those two foolish young women, whose photographs she had good-naturedly burnt, becoming involved? No mud would stick to any of them. None of it would splash devastatingly on to the children. Only the guilty would suffer. So why should anyone criticize her? In a state of quiet satisfaction, she drove homewards to Mark.

H. R. F. Keating

MRS CRAGGS AND THE LIVING DEAD

Once long ago, Mrs Craggs had a job with the greatest newspaper in the world. She was not its Fashion Editor – indeed, in those days it turned up its mighty nose at the notion of anything as frivolous as fashion, let alone a Fashion Editor – but she felt her job was one which had to be done and which contributed its share to the proper conduct of the austere sheet which appeared every morning to be lapped up in clubs and Cabinet offices and places where grave opinions gravely stated count. Mrs Craggs, of course, never read this sheet. She preferred something with pictures. 'Well,' she would say, 'I like a bit o' sauce, an' I don't care who knows it.' Her job on the greatest newspaper in the world was to clean and polish the first floor offices during the mornings when hardly anybody was there. She worked under the general super-vision of Mrs Gollond, the Chief Domestic Assistant. But she herself had no title, resounding or otherwise. And, she sometimes thought, she washed floors and polished them rather better than Mrs Gollond, for all that lady's dis-tinguished office.

One of the things that Mrs Craggs liked best about this job was that nothing ever happened. Her friend, Mrs Milhorne, had a job at the same time on the newspaper which she and Mrs Craggs preferred, and things were different there, if only half what Mrs Milhorne confided to

69

her in the Tube on the way home was true. There, there were sudden sackings and meteoric promotions – 'Why,' said Mrs Milhorne, 'them little name-boards outside their offices, they go up and down so fast it seems like they take them out o' your very 'ands while you're giving them a bit of a dust' – and there were blazing rows and there were reporters coming in at the last second with scoops and murderers wanting to confess and photographs that no one would dare to print, except that they did. But at the greatest newspaper in the world all was always calm. And they had very nice plain brown lino which took polish just a treat.

So it was really quite something to cause a flutter when one morning, as Mrs Craggs and Mrs Gollond were giving the third office on the left as you went down the main corridor a thorough turn-out – 'It's a wonder where all the dust comes from,' said Mrs Craggs. 'We always has dust 'ere,' retorted Mrs Gollond, 'always have and always will' – who should come almost rushing in, insofar as anyone ever rushed in those high-ceilinged offices and corridors, but the Editor himself.

He certainly entered the room abruptly. And then he looked about him as if the presence of the two ladies was altogether unexpected.

But in a moment he recovered himself.

'Ah,' he said. 'Ah. Ah, good morning, Mrs Gollond.'

He knew Mrs Gollond by name. Everyone knew Mrs Gollond by name. She had worked at the paper for longer than almost anybody else. And she made sure that they never forgot.

'Good morning,' she said to the Editor, putting into the words the plain hint that it was now less of a good morning for his having come in and disturbed the rhythm of her task.

'Yes,' said the Editor. 'Yes. Well, you see . . . You see, I was looking for Mr Parmenter. I heard at a dinner last night that the Duke of Holderness is not at all well and I thought that – er – we should be making sure of the obit, you know.'

'I dare say,' said Mrs Gollond.

And she sniffed.

'But that don't alter the fac',' she said, 'that it's not yet gorn half-past ten and it's well known, by me if it ain't by nobody else, that Mr Parmenter don't never come in afore twelve.'

'Oh, yes,' said the Editor. 'Yes, quite. But . . . But I was wondering about young Hipworthy – it is Mr Hipworthy, isn't it? – is he by any chance anywhere about?'

'As fer Mr Hipworthy,' Mrs Gollond pronounced, 'I can't be saying, neither one way nor the other. Mr Hipworthy ain't what you might call regular. Not the way we likes 'em regular here.'

'Well, no. No, I suppose not. A little young, perhaps. Yes, yes. Well, if you do see him, ask him to step round to my office, would you? And good day, Mrs Gollond.'

The Editor smiled, as if it cost him an effort. And then he cast a look in Mrs Craggs' direction.

'Er – good day,' he said.

'Good day, sir,' said Mrs Craggs. 'And we'll be sure to tell him. Don't you worry.'

'Tell him we will or tell him we won't,' said Mrs Gollond as soon as the door was shut, and perhaps just a fraction before. 'Comin' in here at this time. I don't know what he thinks he's thinking of.'

'Well, it was something to do with the Duke of Holderness,' Mrs Craggs said, seeming to be a little less quick on the uptake than she usually was. 'The Duke of Holderness and his obit. Whatever an obit is.'

'An obit,' said Mrs Gollond, speaking with all the authority that her long, long service had imbued her with, 'an obit is what you might call a report an' account of the living dead.'

'Oh, yes?' said Mrs Craggs. 'And what might that be when it's at 'ome?'

Mrs Gollond looked at her, as if it was just possible that she was being disrespectful.

'It's what we writes about 'em when they're gorn,' she explained, as soon as the impossible notion had been swept from her mind. 'We kind o' sums 'em up like. Tells 'em what they did wrong, an' if they did right. An' it's the length what counts, it's the length what counts in the end. Do they weigh up to the full column? Or do they come under it? There's many a man walking the corridors o' Parliament this minute what would wish an' wish with all his might he was going to come up to the full column. But he ain't.'

Mrs Craggs listened to the doom pronounced in her usual impassive manner.

'Ah, well,' she said after a short pause. 'This ain't a-getting Mr Parmenter's desk dusted, nor yet young Mr Hipworthy's table.'

And she turned, whether by way of expressing a prefer-ence which might run dead counter to Mrs Gollond's scale of values or not it was hard to tell, to deal first with the solid but humble corner table allotted to young Mr Hipworthy.

Mrs Gollond advanced on Mr Parmenter's desk, plainly feeling that a due order of precedence was being main-tained. But, hardly had she got to work bundling up the papers on the desk's surface into piles of a neatness and shape which she considered proper, than she stopped with a horrified intake of breath.

'He's done it again,' she announced.

'What? Old Parmenter?'

'Old Mr Parmenter, if you please. Mr Parmenter of the

72

Obituary Department. Leave his keys a-dangling just anywhere he may, but he's Mr Parmenter still. Just so long as
he's in this office. And that won't end all in a minute. Not
'ere, it won't.'

'Why,' said Mrs Craggs, 'won't he go and get the sack
then, for carelessness, leaving his keys the way he does?'

And she innocently polished away at the edge of young
Mr Hipworthy's heavy old table.

'The sack?' said Mrs Gollond. 'The sack? Here? You
don't know what you're talking about, my good woman.
The sack? From this place? Listen, nobody ain't never
been dismissed even from here. Much less get the sack.
Oh dear, oh dear, you ain't got no idea, you ain't. Not no
idea.'

Mrs Craggs went on polishing for a little, working her
way now round the clutter of odds and ends and scraps of
this and scraps of that littering the table. But after a while
she asked another question.

'Not even young Mr Hipworthy?' she said. 'Wouldn't he
even ever get dismissed? The way he goes on? Coming in
at all hours? And playing jokes on people who've been
here long before he so much as saw the light o' day?'

There had been an occasion when young Mr
Hipworthy had glued down a duster which Mrs Gollond
had chanced to leave on his table. And the repercussions
of that had not easily been forgotten.

Mrs Gollond sighed.

'No,' she said, 'not even young Mr Hipworthy, though if
I had my way he'd be the first it'd happen to. The first.'

And there was no doubt that Mrs Gollond thought that
she ought to have her way on the greatest newspaper in
the world.

It was perhaps a good thing it had been that day on which
Mrs Craggs had received instruction on the exact

meaning and moral worth of an obit. Because, just as she was coming out of the back entrance on her way to Blackfriars Underground station, a gentleman approached her and broached that very topic.

'Good day, madam.'

'Good day,' said Mrs Craggs.

She could have said 'Good day, Mr Sundukian' because she had recognised in an instant the portly, spade-bearded, flashing-monocled figure of the notorious, high-living, high-spending financier, Kevork Sundukian. Mr Sundukian's photograph appeared in the newspaper Mrs Craggs favoured almost as frequently as the photographs that bannered the "bit o' sauce" she liked. Occasionally, indeed, the two were conjoined, though Mr Sundukian's bits of sauce always had a whiff of the cultural about them since he was a prodigal outpourer of funds for unusual operatic ventures and for musical events centring on ladies with wonderful voices and dazzling physiques.

But Mrs Craggs just said 'Good day' and waited to see what would happen.

'You work for that splendid journal, I perceive,' said Mr Sundukian, casting a glance at the mellow brick pile behind them.

'Yes,' said Mrs Craggs.

'I envy you, madam. I envy you. I will not disguise from you that I am a wealthy man' – You'd better not, thought Mrs Craggs – 'but I tell you frankly I wish it had been my lot to find an occupation inside those walls. Even of the most simple. Even perhaps the chap who polishes the linoleum there.'

'Well, that ain't a chap,' Mrs Craggs said.

'No, madam?'

'That's me. Or, it is for all the first floor of the place.'

'Ah, I envy you. The first floor. Where I believe the Editor himself has his office. Do you – Tell me, madam, does it fall to you actually to polish the linoleum in that august sanctuary?'

'I don't know about August,' said Mrs Craggs. 'I has my two weeks 'oliday August. But I polishes that floor, yes. And messed up terrible with cigarette burns it is behind the desk there. Terrible.'

'That's sad, madam. Bad even. But, tell me, do you also by any chance have to – er – deal with the office where they file the – ahem – obituary notices?'

'I do,' said Mrs Craggs, who seldom saw any harm in the truth.

'Ah, what a place that must be. What a place. Those accounts of men's lives. Those accounts they will never see, but which the whole world will read the day after their deaths. Remarkable.'

'Could do with a new table in the corner,' said Mrs Craggs. 'Why, the one they got's so old you can't get the dust out of its nooks and crannies, not no how.'

'Indeed? Remarkable. And the filing cabinets, are they equally ancient too? Deficient locks, that sort of thing?'

'No. They locks up all right. It's the chap what keeps the keys that's on the ancient side there. Leaves 'em anywhere, he do. Anywhere.'

'Indeed? Indeed? So I suppose it would not really be difficult for anyone with access to that room at a quiet hour to read a particular "obit" – is that what they call them in the jargon? An obit? – to quietly peruse one of those? Even to – ahem – abstract it?'

'I s'pose you mean pinch it?' said Mrs Craggs.

Mr Sundukian smiled through his great spade of a beard. It was a sudden explosion of charm that had on one particular occasion netted him no less a sum than three-quarters of a million pounds on one single delicate deal.

'Why, yes, madam,' he said. 'You hit it exactly. Would it

be easy enough, if there were a willing agent, to "pinch" a particular obit?'

'Course it would,' said Mrs Craggs.

Mr Sundukian's spade beard opened in another smile.

'Then let me be frank, madam,' he said. 'The obit in question is that of Mr Kevork Sundukian. The agent in question, I devoutly hope, is yourself. And there could be any reasonable sum of money in question, as a consideration. Twenty pounds, shall we say?'

'Take money to do that?' said Mrs Craggs. 'I got more pride.'

Mr Sundukian stopped in his tracks and laid a hand, dashingly manicured, on Mrs Craggs's coat sleeve, threadbare but still ready to keep out a winter's cold.

'Madam,' he said, 'forgive a crass old man. I knew at the very moment I saw you that an approach that mentioned money was out of the question. But I am a financier, madam. I think money. I live money. I cannot help but approach any question in terms of money. Yet I should have known there are people in the world who are better than I am. I should have known that.'

Mrs Craggs blew down her nose, a little like a horse.

'Madam,' said Mr Sundukian, letting go her coat sleeve. 'Allow me to tell you about myself. Let me for once unlock those steel-barred doors that a financier learns to guard himself with from his earliest days. Madam, I am a vain man.'

'Well, o' course you are,' Mrs Craggs agreed.

The spade beard closed then like a great trap. But almost at once it opened again to reveal a smile that was tenderly beguiling, waif-like almost.

'Yes, vain,' sighed Mr Sundukian. 'Vain and anxious. Anxious about what the world thinks of a man who, though he has done his share to make the world a richer place, and more than his share perhaps, is still concerned that he may be thought of, be labelled even, as no more than a machine for making money.'

He paused. He looked at Mrs Craggs.

'Madam,' he said, 'do you see my position?'

'Yes,' said Mrs Craggs, because she did.

'Then, madam, can I dare to hope? I have trodden on your finer feelings with a truly brutal heel. I know it. I regret it. Bitterly. But, madam, can I appeal to those feelings now? Madam, I desire with all the force that is in me to know what that great newspaper will tell the world about me on the day after my death. Madam, will you . . . May I beg you to indulge an old, vain and suffering man?'

'Well,' said Mrs Craggs, looking at the eyes above that spade of a beard which was cut now by the ribbon of a fallen monocle. 'Well, if I could, I would. I tells yer that. But I can't. Yer knows I can't, don't yer? And if I can't, I can't.'

A swift and forcefully manicured hand brought the monocle flashing up to the right eye again.

'A thousand pounds?' said Mr Sundukian.

He got no answer. The monocle twinkled sharply.

'Two thousand?'

The monocle glittered with ferocity.

'Five thousand? Five thousand pounds for that strip of paper?'

The monocled glared.

'Madam, you're a fool. A damned, ignorant, stupid fool.'

And Mr Sundukian jumped into a huge, sliding, gleaming limousine that, at a click of a dashingly manicured hand, had materialized beside him. Mrs Craggs turned towards the Underground.

She decided not to talk to her friend Mrs Milhorne about what had happened. She did not altogether trust Mrs Milhorne's tender susceptibilities.

That might have been that, had it not been for Mrs Craggs's fradgetting over the engrained dust in the nooks and crannies of the old table in the corner of the Obituary Department which was all that young Mr Hipworthy had to call his own. There was one particular packed seam at the top of the thick right-hand leg that had seemed one day as if it was at last going to yield up its riches. It had not quite. But, as Mrs Craggs had been twisting her polishing mop into the cigarette-pocked lino behind the Editor's desk it had suddenly occurred to her that the corner of a duster well moistened with spit might after all do the trick. So she went back to the Obituary office.

And caught Mrs Gollond in the act.

Mrs Gollond had in her hand Mr Parmenter's bunch of keys, which no doubt he had left dangling once again in one of the drawers of his desk, and she had open the big old mahogany-fronted filing drawer on which, in a brass holder, there was a yellowed card bearing the solitary letter 'S'. She had even had one of the long obituary proofs half-way out of its place when Mrs Craggs had opened the door. If Mrs Craggs had stopped to wet the corner of her duster before she had gone in, as she had considered doing, the five-thousand-pound strip of paper might have been in the pocket of Mrs Gollond's flowered apron.

But, as it was, Mrs Gollond simply stuffed it in haste back into its place, slammed the drawer shut and began furiously rubbing at its mahogany surface with her duster.

'I see Mr Parmenter's left his keys again,' said Mrs Craggs.

Mrs Gollond drew herself up.

'He has,' she declared. 'And it's not good enough. There's house rules and there's house rules, and them's what's got to be obeyed. I shall speak to the Editor.'

And that was when Mrs Craggs decided that really and truly it was not good enough. Mrs Gollond had gone too far. It was time something was done.

So, as soon as young Mr Hipworthy came in, she had a quiet word with him.

'I think it's a jolly good wheeze,' said young Mr Hipworthy.

The calm days went by in the offices of the greatest news-paper in the world. The Duke of Holderness died and his updated obituary came to one column and a third, *Services to Agriculture and Philately*. Daily in the Tube on the way home Mrs Milhorne gave Mrs Craggs gory details, of instant sackings, of one Editor for half an afternoon and of what the Crime Reporter had found on his desk – 'I come over so queer I 'ad to go next door for a rum an' pepper-mint' – after an individual in a shabby mackintosh had been allowed incautiously to wait for twenty minutes in his room. But Mrs Craggs had nothing to offer in return.

Till, one day about three weeks later, there was an event that broke the great newspaper's calm in no uncertain manner. Mr Kevork Sundukian entered by the front door flourishing, even brandishing, an enormous whip and demanding to see the Editor.

But of course you cannot horsewhip the Editor of the greatest newspaper in the world any more than you could have cocked a snook at the Prophet Moses. So, after a short interval, all that happened was that a conversation took place between the irate financier and the Editor, the latter flanked as a precautionary measure by the Court Correspondent, who was a former Welsh International Rugby forward, and one of the sub-editors from the Sports Department, hastily summoned and carrying with a certain casualness a cricket bat autographed by the Oxford University team who in 1877 had scored a total of only twelve runs against the M.C.C., an item that had reposed in a corner of the sports sub-editors' room for full many a year. He was a somewhat weedy fellow, but a staunch believer in Wisden's Cricketers' Almanac and a bit of a gossip as well.

It was through him, indeed, that it became known all round the building that the Editor had told Mr Sundukian in round terms that, whether the rather short obituary notice which he had had brought to his attention – *Mr Kevork Sundukian. A Money Making Machine* – was or was not a true copy of what would appear in the paper on the day after Mr Sundukian's decease, 'and, of course, we all – er – hope that will not be for many a long year yet,' it had beyond doubt been obtained by Mr Sundukian in a fraudulent manner and that was absolutely unacceptable.

Mr Sundukian, when on his way out he had been offered back his whip by the young lady from the Advertisement Department's counter into whose safe-keeping it had been put, had donated it, it was reported, to that young lady, but not in a very gracious manner.

Thereafter certain discreet inquiries had been made, by none other than the Manager of the great newspaper himself. In the course of them young Mr Hipworthy had mentioned that he had one evening sketched out a small piece of writing in the form of an obituary and that a friend in the Composing Room had, as it happened, set it up in type. But, he had assured the Manager, now once more in its allotted space in the file marked 'S' there reposed the paper's considered comment, measuring nearly but not quite one full column, on *Mr Kevork Sundukian. Patronage of the Musical Arts.* At the end of the Manager's inquiries Mrs Gollond was peremptorily dismissed, even though dismissals were not very frequent occurrences in the office.

Well, Mrs Craggs had thought when she heard the news, that will be something to tell Mrs Milhorne.

But she did not tell her friend about a short conversation that took place next day. The Editor, coming early into the office, found her twisting and twisting her polishing mop into the cigarette burns on the floor behind his desk.

'Ah – er – yes, Mrs Craggs,' he said. 'Yes. Well, she always was a beastly woman, wasn't she? I'm – er – awfully glad you did what you – er – did.'

Desmond Lowden

THE OLD MOB

Satchel Anderson got up at four that morning. He got his Merc out of the garage and drove off through the suburbs. By half-past four he'd reached the motorway, and by five was approaching the new spur where he was to meet the Geordie. Satchel parked on the hard shoulder and looked across at the floodlights of the twenty-four hour shift. He saw the timber claddings of the piles they were constructing, saw the thick wet cement they were pouring down inside. And then the gravel track he could reverse down, meaning he could get the body out of the boot without getting mud on his Merc.

He drove down to the site hut and got out. But it was then that the first thing went wrong. The Geordie wasn't there. Only his side-kick, the Irishman.

They went inside the hut. The Irishman, bent, cold in his bones and not yet forty-five. He wore a hand-stitched suit covered in white mud. And he had that squint of long eyelids, long upper lip, that came from smoking fags down to the stub.

'Noa, de Geordie, he boggered off,' he told Satchel. 'Boggered off two days back.'

'You're joking,' Satchel said.

'Noa, he went to de ski-ing.'

'Again?'

'Had dis call from him last noit. Cortina di Ampezzo. De

piste is piss poor, he says, piss poor.' The man took a packet of Balkan Sobranies from his pocket. 'Me, oi doan't loik de ski-ing. Not de *apray,* de *avong,* or de *pondong* . . . Noa, oi cruises. Moastly oi cruises.'

'Get away,' Satchel said.

'Now, about dis consignment.' The Irishman put his hand out.

But Satchel shook his head. He knew all about Irishmen in hand-stitched suits, smoking Balkan Sobranies. Irishmen with their hands out. He went away to phone.

London told him to travel east, keep travelling east, and phone in every hour. 'Every *hour?*' Satchel asked. 'Listen, in three hours I'll hit the bleeding sea.'

That was all right, they told him. They wanted him there. What they were working on now was a burial at sea.

The coast bothered Satchel when he arrived. It was flat, grey, with not a dent, not a prick out at sea. The only pricks were on the marshy foreshore, bird-watching pricks maybe, with khaki anoraks and cameras. Satchel drove on, but later he came across more of them, standing in a car park by the road. And the cars behind them all had Press labels. Press, Jesus, that was all he needed with a stiff in the boot.

Satchel drove quicker, putting a lot of miles between himself and the car park. Until, that was, he had the shock that made him swerve off the road. Shock? Series of shocks. Warplanes, huge and spiky, came at him low, about ten feet off the deck. Each one a clap of thunder that flattened the marsh-reeds. Satchel, his hand shaking, switched on the radio, expecting to hear war was declared. But then he remembered. East Anglia, and all that low-level flying. They were on his side.

He started the car again and came to low flat hills. His

map told him they were journey's end, the head of an estuary that wound up from the sea. Ten minutes later he got there. It was a small village. Most of it was mud. And what wasn't mud was little round stones made up into houses, a hotel, a shop, and a yacht chandler's. Stones also made up a wall that went up on the low hill and disappeared over the horizon. Satchel looked at it. He reckoned it had taken a hundred men a hundred years to build that wall.

He parked. In the hotel he found they served six different kinds of malt. In the shop he found paperbacks without any tits on the covers, and Eucryl tooth-powder. And going back outside, he saw something else that exactly fitted into the landscape. Down on the quay a detatchment of the green welly brigade arrived in their Volvo. They stood in a line in their bright green wellingtons. They stared palely down at the mud, told Fiona to stop throwing stones. Then they pissed orf.

And Satchel should have been warned, but he wasn't. He followed instructions and went out on the marshes, driving carefully on a pot-holed track. Then a mast rose ahead of him, just as he'd been told it would, a massive mast, followed by massive spars, and a massive curving deck. It was one of those Thames barges with the wooden flipper-things on the sides. And sitting waiting near the gangplank was the man he'd come here to meet, Darcy.

As soon as he heard Darcy speak, the warning came back. That warning that was ten percent green welly brigade, ten percent Eucryl tooth-powder, and eighty percent stone wall going up over the hill. Because Darcy, he knew in a flash, was no more no less than D'arcy, bl'eeding de'ath with a capital D'. He was as massive as his boat. His sweater, torn and fluffed, went up to a torn and fluffed face. And beneath his taut angry skin was bile that had bubbled since the Middle Ages.

And why, Satchel asked himself, why in God's name had three phone calls to London got him involved with this? The old mob? The real Mafia? The *real* wild boys?

But he knew the answer when Darcy crooked a finger and led him below. It was simple. They were saving money in London. Darcy was poor. He sat like some flaking figurehead against the huge barge timbers, and around him was poverty. There was the paraffin smell from the beat-up Aladdin stoves. There was the damp of the frayed straw-matting. There was junk furniture, and an old portable record-player with the ringmarks of glasses.

Darcy poured himself a tumbler of Scotch and gave Satchel none. 'Ship's captain,' he said then in his voice like a spadeful of gravel. 'Used to be able to marry people, outside territorial waters. And bury them, of course. Legally allowed to dispose of troublesome stiffs. Had high hopes of founding the East Anglian Burial Service once. Considerable undercutting.'

Satchel nodded, trying to kick away a long black dog that was nosing at his crutch.

'Nowadays, different story, of course. I ... *marriage*?' A bark of laughter. 'Always tell people they can surrender to uncontrollable urges on my ship. But the burial part ...' He sucked in his breath. '. . . Only for a *vast* consideration.'

Vast, don't make me laugh, Satchel thought. He fingered the tight roll of twenties in his pocket, the Geordie's pay-packet, the two grand folding which he'd never handed over. It wasn't going to be anything like that here. Casually, Satchel dropped five hundred quid into the talk.

They sparred. Darcy sucking in his breath all the time, and shaking his head. Satchel upping it by fifties. But when he reached seven-fifty, the man started pouring him Scotches.

The sparring went on. The black dog went out, and a woman came in. She was lean and stooping. She had red hair, the kind that shone almost white. And she moved like a ghost, keeping behind Darcy all the time. Suddenly he turned. He shouted at her as soon as he saw her, and went on shouting. Satchel watched her. It was her eyes that bothered him. They shivered, like those old servant-discs used to shiver, in those big old houses when buttons were pressed. Because she was a servant, or Darcy treated her like one. She brought mugs of tea when they had tea-and-Scotch. Gentleman's Relish when they had sandwiches-and-Scotch. Brought them and said nothing.

Satchel got tired of sparring. He thought a moment, then he went up to eight-fifty. His last offer, he said.

'Call it a thou,' Darcy said. 'Extras come into it. I mean, I could say a few words, get out the old union jack.'

'Not for this one.' Satchel nodded in the direction of the bankside, the Merc. 'This one's not British.'

'Oh?' Darcy's eyes were sharp. 'Not your Arab. Your Arab's trouble.'

'No. Black.'

'Blackie, eh?'

'Well, it wasn't really us that handled it,' Satchel said apologetically. 'More like a sub-contract.'

'Blackie,' Darcy repeated. 'Natural sense of rhythm, the Blackie. What if I played some jazz on my clarinet?' He got up then and went past the record-player, showing a clarinet on a stand.

'No.' Satchel spread out his hands. 'No music. Eight-fifty it is, or I go elsewhere.'

'Eight-fifty.' Darcy glanced across to where the woman was standing. 'All right. Game's on.'

The woman spoke, for the first time. 'Game's on, is it?' she asked, a hopeless shrug to her shoulders. 'Loonies, Nil. The Rest Of The World, Nil.'

Satchel didn't understand her. He went to the porthole that looked out on the bandside. And suddenly he stiffened. The black dog was at the boot of the Merc, up on the bumper, sniffing.

'Listen.' He turned. 'Listen, we could have trouble. I mean, it's mild, isn't it? The papers keep on about what a mild winter we're having . . . And that stiff, it should have been in concrete hours ago.'

'Good thinking,' Darcy said. He turned to the woman. 'Get it in the freezer.'

She moved away. Satchel offered to help her, but Darcy said, no, she was your yeoman stock. And she was. Through the porthole they watched her get out the long polythene bundle wound round with insulating tape. She got it up on her shoulder, and, swaying, brought it in over the gangplank.

They followed her, dark ahead of them through the tunnel of the ship. At one point there was a tight corner. A length of the insulating tape came unstuck, and a hand poked out.

Darcy looked at it. 'Thought you said he was black.'

'Well, more coffee-coloured,' Satchel said. 'More Gold Blend.'

The woman made no sound, showed no effort on her face as she rested the body finally by a long chest-freezer.

'Granny-size,' Darcy said darkly, and opened the lid.

He made room, shifting a forequarter of beef and a loin of lamb. Then the woman flipped the body in. The hand came to rest, scooping up frozen peas.

'Could do with a cutlet,' Darcy said, rummaging around. 'Couple of good lean cutlets and some broccoli tips. How about you?'

Satchel pushed the hand back inside the polythene, restuck the tape. 'Don't fancy it myself,' he said.

Lamb-fat glistened on Darcy's chin. 'You know, my mother, God rest her soul, always used to make a cock-up of the French language,' he said. 'Lived in France half her life, yet every time she went to a butcher's shop she asked for *culottes d'agneau*. Lamb's knickers.'

'That so?' Satchel stared at him.

'Fact. Though maybe she knew about it. Certain amount of cunning in our family.' Darcy waved a fork in the air. 'Take her Georgian silver. At the end of her life she had no room for it. She knew we wanted it. She knew she didn't want us to have it. So she solved the whole problem with a stroke of genius. Sent the stuff over from France in the train. Two packing-cases, and she labelled them both Georgian silver.'

Satchel frowned. It wasn't the sort of story he liked to hear, it went against everything he stood for. Then his frown deepened. Suddenly he caught sight of his watch. Four o'clock, Jesus, how many Scotches to the bad was he?

He leaned forward. 'Listen,' he said, 'a couple of hours ago I gave you four hundred and twenty-five quid. The other half to come when you finish. Which I thought was going to be this evening.'

'Darcy shook his head. 'Not a chance.'

'*Not?*'

'Tide's all wrong.'

'That right? When's High Tide then?'

'Oh-nine-thirty-four.'

And it was too quick. He was lying. Satchel looked across at the Scotch bottle, now nearing the end of its natural life.

'You're telling me it's tomorrow then?'

'Tomorrow as ever is.'

Satchel stood up, needing fresh air. 'Where do I go to get a slash?' he asked.

'Out there. First on the right.'

Starting away, Satchel suddenly heard a crash behind him. He turned. Darcy's food-plate lay smashed on the floor. The man was coming at him, reaching out for his pockets. 'Haven't got any Andrex, have you?'

'*What?*'

'Andrex. That tissue stuff. Jams up a ship's loo.' Darcy patted his pockets in turn. 'Surprising the number of people who try to smuggle Andrex in here.'

Satchel went off. He should have been warned, he told himself, should have been bleeding warned.

When he got back, the woman was there, picking up pieces of plate. Darcy had the record-player on, traditional jazz, and was playing along on his clarinet. And it wasn't that he was out of tune, wasn't even that it was all rasping breath and squeaks. It was that he was lurching around, his ears and neck red, and every time he lurched the record missed a groove.

He stopped, and swung round on the woman. 'Keep bloody still,' he shouted.

The woman froze where she was, hand halfway towards a piece of china. Darcy played on, lurched on. The record missed another groove.

Suddenly he went over and clouted her.

She didn't look up at him. 'Loonies, One. The Rest Of The World, Nil,' she said quietly.

Darcy's arm went back again.

Satchel looked at him. He looked on at the empty Scotch bottle. Jesus, he thought, the *energy* of the man. Then he left.

It was getting dark outside, and he was surprised by that. Even more surprised, as he drove back to the hotel in the village, to hear the sounds of drinking, the bar going in and out.

Satchel thought about it. There was only one kind of people could get a drink after hours, he knew. Only one kind of people could raise a large Scotch in a Temperance House in Llanelli. And then he saw them, the Press cars, parked by the hotel. The cars he'd seen earlier out on the marshes, just before the warplanes had come.

Going into the bar, it suddenly all came together. Because the word was, the shouted word, that it was Nato manoeuvres. The word was, that in the next war the West would last two days. That on the third day the only paper to file with would be *Pravda*.

And the word was, there were more manoeuvres tomorrow. Combined manoeuvres, at sea.

The barge-deck throbbed to the sound of the wheezy engine. Darcy spun the wheel and glowered out at the morning. He had his sailor hat on, the black dog was crouching beside him. It was his act, hungover, but still his act.

"preciate your concern, m'dear feller, really do,' he said, unrolling a long tube of cardboard. 'But, see here. We go out in a straight line to the Territorial Limit thingy. And your war-johnnies fart around here. Always do. To the right. The right as you look at the map.'

Satchel had some idea it should be "starboard", and "chart", but he said nothing. They got out of the river without hitting anything. The marsh-reeds fell back behind them, and they wheezed out on a wide silver sea. Darcy got the woman to bring a bottle up on deck. He stoked up on his hangover, overtook it, then got attacks of Charles Laughton and Robert Newton, alternately.

They lasted until he looked at his watch, checked the chart, and cut the engine. The barge slowed up, and fell to slapping and rattling. Darcy moved into the centre of the deck. He looked at the woman and at Satchel. 'There,' he swung an arm round the empty horizon, 'miles and miles of bugger-all.'

Which was when the black tower, the size of four double-decker buses, followed by the black hull the length of two Inter-Cities, suddenly surfaced, close to their right.

'*Piss orf!'s*' Darcy shouted at the nuclear sub.

A huge metal voice came across from the black shape. 'You are in violation of restricted war-zone number six-four-three-stroke . . .'

Men appeared on the deck of the sub, ratings, with rifles.

'Loonies, Three. The Rest Of The World, Five,' the woman said to Darcy.

He swung round and got a large fat-barrelled pistol from a locker. Satchel went for him, but he wasn't at his best, not with the barrel of that pistol by his cheek. He ducked as it went off. A Verey light fizzed up into the air, stuck in the ratlines above, and rained red fire down on them. The dog howled.

Then there was a new sound. A metal launch had come from the sub. It bumped against the barge, and an officer and two ratings held it there. One rating came up over the side. He took the Verey pistol away from Darcy kindly, then hit him kindly, twice, on the face.

Darcy sat down.

The rating moved on to the woman. His voice was conversational. ''kin-ell,' he said. ''kin-Icelandic, is he?'

The woman started to laugh. A slow, strange sound.

The rating came on. 'Not 'kin-Icelandic?' he asked Satchel.

'No. Not that.'

''kin-ecological then? 'kin-Greenpeace?'

'That's it,' Satchel said. 'Greenpeace.'

The rating offered him a Navy-issue fag. ''kin-save the whale,' he said. ''kin-know what you mean. 'kin-Jane Fonda, she's all tied up with your mob, isn't she?'

He lit Satchel's fag and went away to the bows of the

barge. He took a line from the Navy launch and made it fast. Then they were towed, the sub keeping station behind them.

It went on for quite some time. Until there was the sound of a siren, and the tow-line slackened. The rating stubbed out his fag. "kin-shame about Jane Fonda,' he said. 'Always reckoned she had such a good 'kin-body on her.'

He went back to the bows, untied the line, waved at Satchel, and disappeared over the side. The launch disappeared. The sub disappeared. The sea was suddenly flat and grey again, as if nothing had happened.

Darcy, two angry bruises on his face, crawled across the deck to the Scotch bottle.

Satchel kicked it away. 'No,' he said. 'No bleeding more of that. What we do now is wait ten minutes, then we get this stiff out of the freezer and chuck it over . . .'

Three strikes of combat-planes crashed over at mast-height. Satchel threw himself flat. The planes swung in towards the land. White smoke trails ziggered away from them. They did real damage to two hundred square yards of sand, then they swung away and disappeared.

Satchel picked himself up. But suddenly there was another sound, a drone, from out at sea. He turned. The horizon was full of square blocks, black square blocks, with huge bow-waves.

'Start the engine,' he shouted at Darcy. 'Will you just start that bleeding thing?'

But Darcy had got hold of the Scotch bottle again. He was drinking hard. And huffy.

'No,' he said.

'*No?*'

'Put it like this,' the man drank two fingers, then another two fingers, 'can *you* start it?'

Satchel turned towards the engine-hatch, the rusty pipes that were inside it, held together with wire.

'xactly,' Darcy said. He capped the Scotch bottle, hugged it to him. Then he turned. 'Things to settle here.'

He was looking at the woman. And she was crouching on the deck, frightened.

The drone from the sea was now a roar. The black boxes, maybe fifty of them in a line, swept past. Landing-craft, with rows of steel helmets inside them.

Darcy stood huge and mottled in the centre of the deck. 'She *laughed* when that war-johnny called me Icelandic,' he said.

'Oh, come on,' Satchel said. 'I mean. Jesus . . .'

But Darcy went to the woman, stood over her. 'I may have picked you up in some North London ghetto,' he shouted. 'But I've told you, I will not, repeat *not* put up with your Tulse Hill tendencies.'

He swung his arm back, clouted her. 'Loonies, *Four*. The Rest Of The World, Nine,' he screamed. 'Loonies, *Five*. The Rest Of The World, Nine . . .'

Satchel turned away. He saw the landing-craft hit the beach. He saw the assault troops leap out into the surf. They did tricky things with hooks and nylon lines. They swarmed up the sand-cliff and captured the bus shelter at the top. Then they sat down.

'. . . Loonies, *Fourteen*. The Rest Of The World, Nine. Loonies, *Fifteen* . . .'

Satchel went over and stopped it. The woman was clutching her left arm, it had bad bruises on it. Turning, Satchel found a bit of old canvas on a hatch-cover. He made her a sling, and she seemed more comfortable. But it wasn't her arm that bothered him, it was her eyes. There wasn't that flicker of yesterday, that nervousness. They just stared at Darcy with a slow burning hate.

Satchel walked towards him. 'Satisfied?' he asked.

Darcy shrugged.

'So what do we do now?'

'Now,' Darcy said. 'Now I have luncheon.'

'You're joking.'

'Twelve noon.' The man looked at his watch. 'I have a rump steak, I have mushrooms, and . . .' he raised his voice for the woman's benefit, '. . . and I have chips.'

'Chips?' she shouted back at him. 'I can't peel potatoes with one hand.'

'Course you can!' he bellowed. '*Course* you can peel potatoes with one bloody hand!'

She went below. More boats came up . . . but by now Satchel was expecting them, the Press boats, with their cameras at the ready. Darcy posed. And Satchel, crouching out of sight, let him. Jesus, he thought, in another second it'd be David bleeding Dimbleby. In another second it'd be Darcy leaning over the side, shouting, 'War-johnny called me Icelandic. Do I *look* Icelandic? And would you like to see the blackie in the freezer?'

The Press boats went away. Darcy drank Scotch, and gradually mellowed. 'Sorry about that little thingy with the good lady just now,' he said. 'Landlubbers don't know about these things. Different camps set up aboard ship, you see, always two different camps. Something to do with being out at sea. Strain, you know, the loneliness.' He pointed to the maybe two thousand people on the beach.

The rump steak, the mushrooms, and the chips arrived. Darcy ate them cross-legged on the hatch. He drank a little Scotch, played a little clarinet, drank a little more Scotch. Finally he sighed, and went over and started the rusty engine. 'Another day, another dollar,' he said.

And he earned his dollar. Two hours later, with a tiny *plop*, the polythene-wrapped bundle, chained to a forty-pound ballast weight, sank beneath the sea. Satchel paid over the second instalment of £425, and Darcy spun the wheel, heading for home.

There was mist, twilight over the marshes as they drew

level with Satchel's parked Merc. Darcy got the woman to jump on to the bank with a line. She jumped, but then dropped the line, ran off among the reeds. The tide caught the long hull of the barge. It swung out across the estuary. The engine coughed and died.

Satchel expected Darcy to start shouting again. But he didn't. It was the last straw. 'M'dear feller,' he took Satchel's arm, 'don't ever, *ever* go to Tulse Hill.'

Darkness was on them by the time they'd unshipped the dinghy, by the time Darcy had rowed a line across to the mooring-post and back, started the winch. They edged in. Then Satchel looked up.

And saw the two flat-hats getting out of the police car on the bank.

'Nothing to worry about,' Darcy said. 'Dog licence, or some such lunacy. Always these damn creditors turning up. Usually I move on, and they just find these two holes in the bank. I change the ship's name, of course. Make a couple of subtle changes to the superstruct . . .'

But Satchel wasn't listening. Jesus, he thought, it'd better be those war-johnnies, sending someone round to complain.

But it wasn't. The flat-hats led the way below, to the freezer.

'Information laid, Sir,' the tall one said. 'Woman's voice.'

Satchel edged towards the door.

The flat-hat opened the freezer, removed a few plastic bags. And there, where the forequarter of beef should have been, was a dark hand, clutching frozen peas.

Satchel edged further.

'Arabic gentleman, sir,' the flat-hat said.

'*Blast!*' from Darcy.

'Seems to be some signs of mutilation, sir,' the flat-hat said. 'This slice, cut out of the rump.'

Satchel's mouth dropped open.

'And some sort of note, sir. What's it say? "Loonies, Fifteen? The Rest Of The World, Ninety-Three?" '

Satchel ran.

James McClure

PRIVACY FOR BERNADETTE

On the morning of her twenty-first birthday, a very special day in many people's lives, it occurred to Bernadette Johnson that Mummy and Daddy were planning to kill her.

Not that this was so special in itself. They had made at least two other attempts that she could recall: once with a feather pillow placed gently over her face, and once with an excess of sedative in her bedtime cup of cocoa. But these had been impulsive affairs, regretted almost upon the instant, and the threat of extinction had never lasted more than a few seconds.

Whereas it was possibly the very lack of anything impulsive or spontaneous about their present behaviour that had alerted and alarmed her. Their eyes had become evasive, their smiles uneasy, and for the past week or so, it had been noticeable how they avoided making any reference to the future. Furthermore, they seemed curiously detached, as though steeling themselves for something, while at the same time, being intent on keeping up all their usual little attentions.

Taken all in all, the effect was scary.

So scary that Bernadette had at first refused to recognise what was going on, and had told herself it was simply her imagination. But now she'd been confronted, however, by definite evidence of a change in them, by visible proof of their true indifference to her as a person, she was having to admit that her instinctive grasp of the situation was correct. In fact it had all the strength of a genuine premonition.

Bernadette, who felt helpless enough at the best of times, wept a little, believing she was powerless to stop them.

'There, there,' said Mummy. 'Tears on your birthday? We can't have that, Bernadette!'

'Tears of joy,' said Daddy. 'Am I right, my love? It's all these lovely cards and presents.'

He was right: it was largely the cards and presents.

Nasty cheap cards, all blue birds and trashy verses; not one of them fit to stand on her bedside table. And as for her presents, just look at them.

A box of her favourite milk chocolates. A bottle of her favourite fizzy drink. A box of those heavenly sweets with the syrupy centres. And, oh bliss, a huge bunch of soft bananas. All well and good, but what about the things you were meant to keep? A pink bedjacket that smelled musty with age; two china dogs with dust in their creases, and finally, to mark this day of days, a slightly tarnished wristwatch that came without a case. When compared to the gifts she'd received in previous years, this collection of old tat off a market stall was enough to give anyone a sinking feeling.

'There, there,' said Mummy, leaning over to dab the tears away with a tissue. 'Twenty-one today! Just fancy that!'

'Doesn't seem possible,' said Daddy.

'How true,' said Mummy. 'It seems like only yesterday we stood by your cot on your very first birthday, and that dimply little smile of yours hasn't altered one bit!'

'Nothing's changed,' said Daddy.

What utter rubbish. Bernadette could see changes all

right, even if her memories didn't go as far back as that. Daddy stooped and grey, his trousers baggy now and his face all sharp creases; Mummy as skinny as a sparrow's legs, watery-eyed and tottery, with breasts like hot water bottles.

'Happy birthday!' said Daddy, giving her a kiss that smelled revoltingly of his white stomach medicine.

'Happy birthday!' said Mummy, giving her a quick peck that left a smear of spit she couldn't wipe off.

Bernadette dimpled, hoping this would get rid of them. It wasn't simply that she desperately needed time to think. People became really disgusting as they aged, and it only made things worse when circumstances were such that they had to keep touching you.

'Well,' said Daddy, glancing at Mummy.

'Well,' said Mummy. 'Now you just lie there like a good little girlie, while we go and see to a very special breakfast for you.'

No mention of many happy returns.

'We love you,' they said together, pausing in the doorway, smiling uncertainly.

The hypocrites! No wonder they weren't too confident that she'd be taken in by such nonsense. Bernadette had never loved, but she'd seen what it was really like on the telly.

'You do the bacon, dear,' Mrs Johnson said to her husband in the kitchen. 'My poor old eyes have terrible trouble trying to cut the rind off.'

'Not that mine are much better, dear!'

'At least you won't waste as much.'

Mr Johnson opened the refrigerator door. 'Those tears,' he said. 'They were awful.'

'Dreadful,' agreed Mrs Johnson, breaking an egg into a mixing bowl.

101

'I fear she was disappointed. She must have been expecting something very special to mark the occasion.'

'Perhaps we should go out and buy her something. We could say we'd kept it back as a surprise.'

'But what with?'

'I know,' sighed Mrs Johnson.

'Just the bananas cost nearly a pound.'

'I know, I know,' said Mrs Johnson, taking up her egg whisk. 'Mind you, I still say that everything we found for her was as good as new, and far nicer than anything we could've afforded. Why, I don't think I ever had that dear little watch on my wrist, not with all the continual washing I've had to do.'

'Mint condition,' confirmed Mr Johnson, 'and most appropriate too, considering the reason I presented it to you, all of twenty-one years ago!'

Mrs Johnson smiled fondly. 'Don't forget to close the fridge door, dear,' she reminded him.

'She wasn't too taken with her cards either,' said Mr Johnson, seeing to the door. 'It was there in her face. But if we'd bought one of those great big expensive ones, what would we have done for the others we pretend come from family and friends? They don't grow on trees!'

'If only,' said Mrs Johnson, 'we could explain to her how difficult things've become. About you being on a pension now.'

'And what inflation is doing to it.'

'But we can't.'

'No, it would only frighten her,' said Mr Johnson.

He bent low over the kitchen table to trim the rind from two rashers of bacon. His wife whisked the egg clumsily, splashing some on her apron.

'You were perfectly right, you know,' murmured Mr Johnson. 'Nothing's altered. She's still very much our big chubby baby.'

'I didn't mean it quite that way!'

'Nevertheless, still in the nursery.'

'Hush, you mustn't —'

'Still can't lift a finger to fend for herself.'

'There is *some* movement in that right arm.'

'Still needs her nappy changed.'

Frugally, Mrs Johnson held her whisk over the bowl to catch the last drips. 'Oh, when one thinks of the years! Those long, long years . . .'

'And of the years to come,' said Mr Johnson, feeling the edge of the kitchen knife. 'Do you think she suspects anything?'

Now that the shock of full realisation had died away somewhat, Bernadette found herself able to see things from her parents' point of view.

It even made sense why all this should have coincided with her twenty-first birthday. In having to mark the occasion, they must have been forcibly reminded of all the years they'd given up to nurturing what amounted to an eternal cuckoo in their nest. Nearly a quarter of a century gone by, and yet they had nothing to show for it, other than the toll it had taken on them, nor would they ever achieve anything.

Bernadette knew she had no illusions about herself. She was gross, useless, capable of producing nothing beside waste matter, and what was more, a freak of nature that should have been destroyed at birth. The only wonder of it was that her parents had retained their own illusions for so long, before being stripped of them and left to see her as she really was. This she found totally perplexing. But for the rest, she considered it entirely understandable that they would want to rid themselves of this obscenity while a little time remained to them, just as it was perfectly natural that they would want to avert their eyes from then on.

Such insights did not, however, breed sympathy. Bernadette realised that she hated them for allowing things to come to this pass, when once again it was they who would dictate her fate, as they had done every second of the past twenty-one years. She hated them for giving her life, and she hated them for thinking they had the right to take it away again. She hated them most of all, perhaps, for not having had the guts to just kill her on first impulse, so that death would have come to her completely without warning.

But no, in order to protect themselves, they were awaiting exactly the right moment, and this meant that she, knowing what she now knew, would have to wait too, dying a thousand deaths until it finally happened.

Her right hand feebly contracted, turning into a loose fist.

Bernadette noticed this and smiled. Her instincts were showing her the way again.

'What's this I hear?' asked Sister Catchpole, the district nurse, all bustle and big silver buckle. 'You won't touch your breakfast? Why ever not?'

Bernadette eyed her carefully, never having been quite sure of whose side she was on. The huge flushed face, framed by fluffy ginger hair, seemed stern, that was all.

'Please yourself,' said Sister Catchpole, opening her black bag to remove a pair of disposable plastic gloves. 'It's high time we tried to get some of our weight down, but your poor parents obviously went to some trouble, and I do think you could have at least made an effort to eat a little of it.'

And then, without further ado, and before Bernadette had a chance to decide exactly what to make of that remark, Sister Catchpole drew back the bedclothes and said briskly, 'Right, with a quick heave-ho, we're turning over on our tummy now.'

Finding her face suddenly sunk in her feather pillow, Bernadette suffered an instant of sheer panic.

'I didn't time that very well, did I?' chuckled Sister Catchpole. 'No sooner do I take off your Conti pad than you wet the sheet! Never mind.'

Bernadette muffled a sob in her pillow, then turned her head for some air, trying not to gasp. It dismayed her to discover how easily she could lose control, especially when keeping calm and collected was probably essential to her survival.

'Our buttocks,' observed Sister Catchpole, tut-tutting, '*are* in a sorry state this morning. They're going to take a while to tidy up, I'm afraid, but I won't be a second longer than I have to.'

That seemed to show a caring concern, but Bernadette wasn't going to reveal what she knew until she felt certain that Sister Catchpole would help her. So she just lay there, feeling nothing, while the treatment was carried out. There was the crackle of paper being torn from packs of sterilised gauze and dressings. The repeated clink of forceps against the inside of a kidney bowl. The sound of the special sticky film being stripped from its roll, and the snick of scissors cutting it to size.

'That's done,' said Sister Catchpole eventually. 'And now let's get ourselves in a fit state to receive visitors.'

Bernadette was rolled this way and that. Sister Catchpole was an expert at bed baths, and pried into every corner with her flannel. She replaced the wet sheet, plumped up the pillows, and arranged everything neatly.

'Our fingernails need cutting again,' she told Bernadette, 'but I think we can safely leave that till tomorrow.'

Tomorrow? Nothing could be safely left until tomorrow!

At her bedside, Bernadette had a Possum; a patented

device that enabled even those paralysed from the neck down to perform a range of simple tasks, all by just blowing or sucking through a tube. She closed her lips over the mouth-piece, gave a sharp puff to activate her alphabet panel, and lit up a series of letters in swift succession.

H–E–L–P M–E

Sister Catchpole frowned. 'Of course I'll help you with them,' she said. 'You do seem to be acting a little strangely this morning! First your breakfast . . .'

F–O–O–D M–I–G–H–T B–E P–O–I–S–O–N–E–D

'Sorry, pet,' said Sister Catchpole, distracted by packing away her things. 'I'm afraid I missed that. What was it again?'

F–O–O–D

Bernadette broke off abruptly. Daddy had just entered the room, carrying a fresh towel.

'Food?' said Sister Catchpole. 'So we've decided we're hungry after all! You can be a little madam.'

'I can't face breakfast myself sometimes,' said Daddy, winking at Bernadette. 'Don't worry, my love, I'll bring you through something in a minute!' And then he enquired of Sister Catchpole, 'How were we this morning?'

'Our tail still isn't too bright.'

'Oh dear – and our legs?'

'Much, much better. The nasty rash has all gone, almost.'

'That's good news! Seen all our cards and things?'

'Oh yes, they're lovely – such a pretty little watch. If you wear it on your right arm, Bernadette, it'll encourage you to exercise it more.'

'Now there's an idea,' said Daddy. 'Could the wife and I tempt you to a small sherry, Sister? By way of celebration?'

'I'd love to, but I really can't, Mr Johnson – must rush. Bye for now, my pet! Be good.'

Sister Catchpole started towards the door, allowing

Daddy to carry her bag for her, as he always insisted on doing. In another moment, she'd be gone.

'N–no!'

Daddy and Sister Catchpole spun round. Their eyes narrowed; their mouths set in a hard line. Each looked at Bernadette in exactly the same cold, frightening way. There was nothing to choose between them.

'Na–na–no–nunny–nuck–nuck.'

'Just for a moment . . .' said Daddy.

'I thought so too,' said Sister Catchpole.

'*Did* you say something, Bernadette?'

'Nuck–nuck,' she uttered, dimpling.

Sister Catchpole and Daddy smiled back, glanced at one another, and went out, still smiling.

God, that had been close. Only just in the nick of time had Bernadette been lucky enough to have it confirmed whose side the old bitch was on.

'You look shaken, dear,' said Mrs Johnson to her husband, when he came into the living-room after seeing the district nurse to her car. 'Whatever's the matter?'

Mr Johnson took out his pipe to fiddle with. He hadn't allowed himself any tobacco for ages, not at the price it was today, but whenever he became agitated, that pipe would find its way into his hand.

'Well?' prompted Mrs Johnson, stopping in the middle of the floor with the carpet cleaner. 'Is it what we've feared?'

He nodded. 'Sister says those pressure sores on her bottom are now big enough to hide oranges in. She's almost worn right through to the viscera.'

'Viscera?' queried Mrs Johnson.

'She can't go on being treated for them at home. She has to go in. It could involve surgery.'

'Why not come out with that straight away? It's no more

than what Sister had warned us might have to happen.'

'I don't know,' said Mr Johnson, shrugging. 'It's a hard thing to finally accept, I suppose – even harder to tell her.'

'Sister's already offered to do that.'

'But we always promised we'd never allow her to be taken away from us, not while we're both still alive and kicking. If things are as bad as they think, she isn't likely to come out again. They'll have to keep her there.'

Mrs Johnson's hand went to her lips. 'Bernadette's not having to go in today, is she? The whole reason for keeping the possibility of this from her was so that her birthday wouldn't be spoiled! Is that why you're –'

'No, not today. At the weekend, she said.'

'So we don't have to let her know right away?'

'Wouldn't dream of it.'

'Thank goodness for that,' said Mrs Johnson, but her eyes remained fixed on the pipe. 'There must be something else you haven't –'

'That was all Sister said.'

'But you're like a leaf!'

'Am I?'

'No secrets now! We've never had any secrets in this house, not so far as Bernadette is concerned.'

Mr Johnson crossed the room to tap the face of his retirement clock on the mantelpiece. 'Hardly worth mentioning,' he said. 'I see it's lost another minute.'

'Let me be the judge of what's worth mentioning. Go on.'

'Well,' he said reluctantly, 'just as Sister was leaving, I could've sworn she said something.'

'And so?' said Mrs Johnson, bemused.

'Bernadette, that is.'

'Bernadette *spoke?*'

'It was only an impression, although Sister –'

'But she couldn't have! She lost her speech at fourteen!'

'Quite so,' said Mr Johnson, leaving his pipe on the mantelpiece where the china dogs had once stood. 'As I say, it was only an impression. She made one of her occasional noises, and we both mistook it for a word. A pure accident, a fluke – call it what you will.'

Pale, Mrs Johnson sank into the chair beside the telephone. 'And is that what Sister thinks too?'

'Apparently. We didn't discuss it.'

'Remember her saying that it might not be genuine dumbness? What was that she called it? You're the one who's learned all the right long words to use.'

'Elective mutism,' said Mr Johnson.

'Yes, that.'

'To be frank, for a moment there, I wasn't at all sure Sister was wrong. It gave me quite a turn.'

'I should think so,' said Mrs Johnson.

'But that was me being ridiculous, even spiteful.'

'Of course it was,' Mrs Johnson agreed firmly. 'Bernadette couldn't possibly be so cruel as to pretend a thing like that.'

'By the way, dear, she's decided she would like a spot of breakfast after all. Shall we go through and –'

'Nobody could be so cruel,' said Mrs Johnson, trembling. 'Not when she knows full well how I've ached these past seven years to have a proper conversation with her, the way we used to do. And how I'd give anything to hear her call out "Mummy" again, instead of just ringing that dreadful bell.'

'She'll be ringing it soon enough,' joked Mr Johnson, 'if we don't go and do something about her breakfast. Or is it brunch by now?'

'If I thought she'd done that to me,' said Mrs Johnson, twisting a yellow duster in her workworn hands, 'I don't know what I'd do. I'd – well, I'd want to kill her!'

'I knew I shouldn't have said anything,' sighed Mr

Johnson. 'Especially as there isn't the slightest reason for you to get yourself worked up like that.'

Our buttocks, thought Bernadette, still with the hateful smell of Sister Catchpole around her. Our legs, our arms, our tummy, our weight, our fingernails ... It was bad enough not having a scrap of ordinary privacy, but not even her own body was hers and hers alone.

Everyone had a share in it, and a bigger share than she'd ever have, if you considered how many more things they were able to do with it than she could. Wash it, move it, paint it red or strangle it, they were the ones with the choices. While she lay there, trapped inside its dead weight, watching them come and go, treating her at best like an open book, or at worst, sampling her blood and telling her how fascinating her disease was.

Small wonder she felt so vulnerable, so totally exposed, so painfully *public* and in desperate need of some secret, known only to herself, that she could cling to. Small wonder, she told herself, that in the end she'd had to contrive one, even if it'd meant choosing not to do one of the few things she could do.

'*My* arm,' whispered Bernadette, and giggled.

Then she tried moving it again, hoping that there was sufficient strength in those slack muscles for her to defend herself. But the arm obeyed her commands all too slowly, and then refused to travel over to protect her left side, which was nearest the door. She could touch the tip of her nose, that was all.

Undaunted, she turned her attention to the hand on the end; that hand which had closed into a fist and urged her to fight back. Provided it could grasp something sharp, and provided she could manage one short, jerky move-ment, then her chances of beating off, say, another faceful of pillow, were really quite reasonable. It didn't take her long, however, to find out that its grip was very weak. The heaviest thing it could lift was the flimsy oxygen mask that was kept beside her bed in case of a bad asthma attack.

'Blast,' said Bernadette.

That left only the Possum as a possible line of defence. She closed her lips on the mouthpiece and ran it through what it could do. She switched on the television set; she opened and closed a window; she opened and closed her curtains; she put the lights on and off; she linked the alphabet panel to her electric typewriter and tapped out SOS, but there wasn't any paper between its rollers.

'SOS!'

Now there was a brilliant idea. As soon as it grew dark, she could try signalling with her room lights. Someone across the road would read the message, realise it was a May Day call, and come flying over to rescue her!

'Rubbish,' said Bernadette.

Who would ever believe her story? The whole street did nothing but praise her parents to the skies, calling them sickening things like "saints" and "perfect angels", quite ignoring how angelic *she* had to be to keep from screaming when they slobbered kisses on the side she couldn't reach. And that was her parents' overwhelming advantage, of course; the fact that nobody, no matter who, would ever credit for one moment that they really had murderous intentions towards their "dearly beloved" handicapped daughter.

'God, how unfair,' muttered Bernadette. 'There's only me on my side – one against them all.'

There was a tinkle. She looked round and saw Mummy standing there with a tray of breakfast things. Whether she had slipped into the room in time to hear that, there was no way of knowing. Mummy's smile wasn't very pretty though.

Mr Johnson looked up in surprise from his crossword puzzle on the kitchen table. 'She guzzled that lot down fast enough!' he said, nodding at the tray.

'She wouldn't touch a morsel of it,' said Mrs Johnson, very quietly. 'I coaxed her into a little of her fizzy drink, that was all.'

'Good heavens! What is she playing at today?'

'I'm sure I don't know – would you like this one too?'

'No, you have it, dear. You haven't had bacon in ages either.'

'I couldn't.'

Mr Johnson rose and took the tray from her, noticing how pale she'd become again. 'You poor lass,' he said tenderly. 'You look very overwrought.' He set the tray down on the draining board. 'It isn't right that Bernadette should be acting up in this way.'

'She –'

'Yes, go on. Let's hear it.'

Mrs Johnson shook her head.

'But it's time you stopped bottling so much up,' he said, taking her awkwardly in his arms and pulling her withered cheek against his shoulder. 'Don't think I've never noticed.'

Such a warmth of sympathy was too much for Mrs Johnson. In moments, she was crying.

'You've stood all you can take,' he said, patting her on the back. 'And I've stood all I can take. It's right that she is going.'

'Don't. Don't say that.'

'I'm only being honest.'

'The fault was ours. Late marriages –'

'Bah!' said Mr Johnson.

'But it's true, it's proven. It's part of the risks of childbirth after forty.'

He eased her away from his to look her in the eye.

'Admit it,' he said. 'Admit that as soon as Sister mentioned the chance of her going into hospital, everything changed. Became more difficult.'

'I – I've had to try not to love her so much. I couldn't bear to part with her otherwise.'

'Is that really the case?' asked Mr Johnson, his voice gruff and shaky. 'Or was it that you didn't *have* to love her any longer?'

'Meaning what?'

'If we didn't think we loved her, would we have gone through with it? Tolerated all her nasty little ways? Who knows? Perhaps, over the years, we've even grown to hate her.'

Very shocked, Mrs Johnson drew away from him. 'However can you say such a thing!'

'It could be true. We've had our momentary lapses.'

'God forgive you.'

'He's never shown much interest!'

'And on her twenty-first birthday too . . .'

'Yes,' said Mr Johnson. 'Do you know what a twenty-first birthday means to most parents? It's the day you get shot of your kids. The day they become fully adult and stride off into the world. What does ours do?'

'I can't listen to any more of this. Whatever's come over you?'

But Mr Johnson kept his hold on her. 'I'll tell you what she does. She lies there, sneering at her presents, and then, thinking it funny, she has us running up and down with trays of breakfast she doesn't want – and it's not as if she can't see we're getting on in years either!' Then he too began to cry, biting hard on his lower lip and ashamed to be so unmanly.

This brought a change to Mrs Johnson, who moved back into his arms, clutched his lapels and said, 'Don't, please don't! You've always been what's most precious to me, and I can't bear to see her doing this to you.'

'S—sorry, it's just . . .'

'I tell you what,' said Mrs Johnson, 'why not go down to the pub for a pint this lunch-time? Give yourself a bit of a treat! It must be months since you last saw any of your cronies, and I know what they used to mean to you.'

'But I can't leave —'

'Oh yes, you can. I can manage on my own perfectly well.'

'Beer's gone up terribly since —'

'Take some of our emergency money.'

'I couldn't do that!'

'Take the money, dear,' said Mrs Johnson, very firmly. 'To be frank, I could do with you out of the house for a few hours. There is something I've got to see to.'

Hunger was making Bernadette very uncomfortable, and she looked longingly at the bananas on her bedside table. Unlike a bottle of fizzy drink, however, which wouldn't fizz if anyone had been tampering with its contents, there was no way of telling if the bananas hadn't been injected with something or other.

Perhaps it was hunger which had also brought her mood so low, for the fight seemed to have gone out of her.

Fight! That was a joke. She had been wracking her brains for hours, but she still hadn't the slightest idea of how someone in her position could defend herself. What added to her anxiety was the fact this couldn't go on indefinitely: sooner or later she would *have* to accept some of their food or drink, and take a terrible chance doing so.

She looked round her room. Well, it was known as her room, but it wasn't as though she'd had much to do with its decoration or arrangement. All she really saw were the walls, papered with a faded floral pattern, closing in on her.

114

This trapped feeling triggered off an old memory that made her shudder every time it came to mind. The memory was that of an article in the local newspaper just before Christmas one year. A couple had been watching the television in their lounge, when a plastic Christmas tree in the corner had caught fire, set ablaze by faulty wiring in its fairy lights. The couple had put out the fire without much trouble, and then had gone on to watch the rest of the programme, before finally going up to bed. There they had found their two toddlers lying dead in their cots, killed by the fumes from one little plastic Christmas tree, wafting up the stairs. This had taken place in Oxford, so far as she remembered, and the coroner there had said he was amazed such a tragedy could happen. But a fire officer had told the inquest that it didn't take much to kill someone with smoke, a couple of smouldering blankets or as few as eight burning news-papers would do it. For a long time after coming across this story, Bernadette had lived in terror of her father accidentally setting fire to something with his pipe, and of the dreadful moment when she'd see the smoke come creeping in through her ever-open doorway.

'Bernadette,' said Mummy, appearing in that doorway, 'I've come to give you one last chance of explaining your attitude this morning.'

Bernadette pretended she was asleep.

'You're not asleep,' said Mummy. 'You didn't close your eyes fast enough to fool me.'

Bernadette went on pretending to be asleep.

'Just as you weren't quick enough about something else earlier on. I'm sure you know what I mean.'

Her voice had a very scary edge to it, so Bernadette slyly opened one eye to see if she was carrying anything. She was not.

'You can talk, can't you, Bernadette?'

She made no response.

'Not that it really matters any more,' said Mummy, giving a strange crooked little smile, 'as you'll find out tomorrow.'

Then her mother turned and vanished from the room, leaving Bernadette with her right hand again closed in a fist, and her heart beating wildly.

So that was their plan! Get her birthday over with first, just in case family or friends dropped in unexpectedly, and then carry out their plot to kill her. They had given more thought to all this than Bernadette had suspected, which in turn suggested that poisoning her food would have been considered too crude and risky. No doubt they had some form of fatal accident in mind; something they could never be blamed for.

How hard her fist had become; it was hurting.

A fist . . .

Just how stupid could she be? Fists weren't a symbol of defence, but of attack!

'Right,' muttered Bernadette, looking afresh at the lethal potential of the objects around her, 'so I've got until tomorrow – you shouldn't have let that slip, you know . . .'

Mr Johnson came home drunk from the pub at a quarter past three. To begin with, he was very cheerful, and insisted on Mrs Johnson sharing a small sherry with him.

'Lovely lads,' he said. 'Lovely lads – all sent their best, by the way.'

'That's nice,' said Mrs Johnson.

'Quite a celebration.'

'Really?'

'Well, you know, our baby's twenty-first. Swore they'd have sent cards if they'd known.'

'That's nice.'

'Restored their faith, they said.'

'What did?'

116

'Y'know, you and me. How we'd soldiered on, never once complaining. One in a million, they said. Others would have long since called in the fella from the knacker's yard.'

Mrs Johnson winced. 'I'm glad you had a happy time,' she said uncomfortably. 'Was it cold out?'

'Freezing. Fancy another drop?'

'One's my limit, dear.'

'Can't say it makes you very chatty! Or is something the matter?'

'It's best left for later.'

'No secrets, Mrs J!' said Mr Johnson, wagging a finger. 'Who was it who said that only this morning?'

'Well,' replied Mrs Johnson, fiddling with her glass, 'while you were out, I saw to that little matter I mentioned. I rang Sister and demanded that Bernadette was admitted immediately.'

'You did *what?*'

'I asked if she could go in today. I don't want her in the house a minute longer.'

Mr Johnson swayed to his feet. 'I hope you didn't do that on my account,' he said, appalled. 'I've had time to think over things, and perhaps –'

'Bernadette can speak,' interrupted Mrs Johnson. 'She's obviously been able to speak all along. It's simply that she doesn't consider we're fit people to speak to.'

'Now who's been telling you –'

'I heard her myself.'

'The little bitch!' said Mr Johnson, sitting down with a bump. 'That's it! That is the very end. If she's not out of here by tonight, I won't be responsible for my actions!'

Mrs Johnson nodded at the telephone. 'Sister thinks today is out of the question, but tomorrow they ought to be able to take her. She was going to check on the bed position and should be ringing back any minute now.'

The ever-open doorway had provided the basis for Bernadette's brilliant inspiration. Instead of imagining the smoke creeping in, she'd suddenly imagined it creeping out.

And while working out the rest of the details, she talked away happily to herself. 'These woolly blankets won't be too difficult to pull off – great, they're not tucked in too tightly. They can go into that horrid enamel bucket they always keep beside me, and then they'll burn without burning anything else. I can make a start on scrunching up pages from magazines for kindling, and hide them under my pillow on the right. Or could I manage to tip over that bottle of surgical spirit? It might be worth trying. Now how will I light it? I know, there's bound to be a box of matches about for the candles on my cake, and I'll find a way of getting hold of them. Good, something to burn, something to light it with, and Possum can see that my windows and curtains are shut. I'd best wait until they fall asleep, of course, and to put them off their guard, I'll be as nice as I can to them.'

Then it struck Bernadette that her plan had a fatal flaw: it was all very well imagining the smoke creeping out of the door, but what about its effects on her before that?

A funny law seemed to influence really good plans, for no sooner did a problem present itself, than a solution arrived hard on its heels. A special lever had been fitted to the oxygen tank on its stand at the head of her bed; a really long lever that her father had designed so that the weight of her right arm was sufficient to turn on the flow of gas, should she suffer an asthma attack when there was nobody in the room to help her. She'd never actually used it – her parents had always arrived in time – but she knew from the trial runs that it worked perfectly. And so, while Mummy and Daddy succumbed to the fumes, she could lie there in her mask, safe as houses.

That left only one thing that could go wrong. Suppose they decided not to bring up her cake and light its candles?

Sister Catchpole did not ring back. She came round to the house at five and told Mr and Mrs Johnson that a bed would not be available for at least another week. There was now a porters' strike on at the hospital, and only real emergencies were being admitted.

'This is a real emergency,' growled Mr Johnson, with half a bottle of sherry inside him. 'Can't you see what this is doing to the wife?'

Mrs Johnson was sitting hunched in a dark corner of the living-room.

'It's because I appreciate the shock and stress involved that I thought I'd stop by instead of just ringing,' said Sister Catchpole, taking a seat. 'I want to explain to you what elective mutism means – it happens sometimes when children have to be left in hospital, and they think their mothers have rejected them – and I want you to try and see this business of a twenty-first birthday from Bernadette's point of view. For example, I deliberately played it down this morning.'

'Played it *down?*' said Mr Johnson.

'Well, wouldn't it make you broody to have everyone celebrating your adulthood, when you haven't the slightest chance of ever being a real adult? And you know how touchy and super-sensitive Bernadette can be at the best of times! There's a lot we must discuss, my dears.'

Mr Johnson was very mauldin by the time Sister Catchpole rose to leave. 'Our poor, poor baby,' he kept lamenting, wiping his eyes with his tie.

'Now don't go saying that in front of Bernadette, for heaven's sake!' warned Sister Catchpole. 'You're just to act perfectly naturally, ignore the mutism, and go ahead with the little party you'd planned for her – if you don't, that might upset her too. I'm sure it'll all go off far better than you expect, you know! We've got rid of a lot of our tensions.'

And she was right. It was a lovely little party, and afterwards Mr and Mrs Johnson said they'd be eternally grateful to Sister Catchpole. Then they retired, emotionally worn out.

'Fattening me up for the kill, were you?' giggled Bernadette, pleasantly surprised by how early her parents had gone to bed. 'But you shouldn't have given Baby a rattle, you know! Not even if she liked the pretty picture of a ship on it.' And she hugged the box of matches to her, feeling very wicked.

Daddy's snores were the first to reach her, a little louder than usual. Then came Mummy's, accompanied by that curious clicking sound, probably made by her dental plate. Each steadied into a definite rhythm.

On reflection, Bernadette didn't feel exactly wicked – it surely wasn't wicked to strike back in self-defence – but *alive,* more alive than she'd ever been.

For a while, she just lay there, enjoying this sensation. Then she looked at the watch that Daddy had strapped to her right wrist, and wondered if it wasn't time that she started her preparations. They could easily take her an hour or more.

They took two.

But at last, all was in its place, and the moment had arrived to drop a lighted match into the bucket.

'Ready?' said Bernadette, sweaty with excitement.

Then she hesitated, suddenly afraid that she might have got everything wrong, and that, despite all the evidence, her parents had no intention of killing her. If she took their lives, it would of course mean her having to go into a home of sorts, where she'd not have a room of her own, and where she'd have to put up with all kinds of strangers.

Actually, having made herself face up to this prospect, the idea rather appealed to her. Privacy was something that would never be hers, no matter where she was, but at least she'd have a bit of life around her, a bit of variety, young people to attend to her needs, and nobody planting great smelly kisses.

So right or wrong – and who was it that'd said she'd never be allowed to go into a home while they were alive and kicking? – her instincts had been, as usual, unerring.

She lit a match at her first attempt, dropped it into the bucket, saw the flames leap up, fed by the spirit, and then, very calmly, she placed the plastic oxygen mask over her nose and mouth, before allowing her arm to drop onto the lever.

The mask slipped. Her hand returned to it, made an adjustment, and then stayed there, ensuring her safety.

Mr Johnson groaned, stirred and raised his head.

At first, he muzzily supposed that his terrible dream had awoken him, and that the sensation of having hydrochloric acid squirted down his throat would quickly pass. Then he realised that his dream and reality had become confused, and that he was in fact suffering from acute heartburn. Not that he deserved any better after all the drinking he'd been doing.

He was pleased his movements hadn't disturbed Mrs Johnson, whose turn it was to sleep with the ear plugs that night, while he was' on duty, as it were, to see to Bernadette's needs.

Tiptoeing, he crossed the landing into the bathroom, where he took down his bottle of white stomach medicine. He swallowed a tablespoonful of it, grimaced, and tiptoed out again. He noticed a strange glow coming from his daughter's room.

Half-asleep, still with his head filled by horrible images of his wife under torture, her tongue torn out and her poor heart bleeding, he went into the old nursery. What he saw there seemed to be part of the same nightmare, although on another level, the cold logic of the arrangements made immediate sense to a former insurance claims adjuster.

For a moment, conditioned by years of caring, Mr Johnson was about to apologise for the fact that the oxygen cylinder was virtually empty, and that he'd quite forgotten to fit a new one.

Instead, he tiptoed out of the room and closed the ever-open door behind him.

Jennie Melville

WHAT I TELL YOU TWICE TIMES TWO IS TRUE

Nora first had serious thoughts of turning to crime while she was in prison. The wrong way round, you might think, the horse running well after the cart, but not so, Nora said she was in prison unfairly. She was innocent. She should not have been there. She said so to her cell-mate. 'I shouldn't be in here.'

'Nor me, neither,' said Baby promptly. She had a real sense of grievance. Once, it was true, Baby had been part of a group of four women criminals, of whom one was dead, another living alone in London (having served her sentence) and the third, Phil, who had been Baby's close friend, had cut loose and disappeared on her own. For the crimes of robbery with violence of which they had undoubtedly been guilty only one of them, Bee, had gone to prison, while Baby and Phil had escaped unscathed. It was, therefore, galling, although perhaps poetically just, that Baby should have been sent to prison for shop-lifting when she was not guilty. She said the police were determined to get her for *something*.

'Well, *I* am innocent,' said Nora, almost as if she did not believe in her companion's innocence, but Baby decided not to take it up. 'It was a fix. I was made to seem guilty. Well, right then! I'm going to get my own back. If they want a criminal, they can have one. Wait till I get out.'

'If you think it's a good idea,' said Baby, doubtfully.

'I do.' Her voice was grim. 'What about you?'

'I'm keeping my options open.'

'It was the way it was done to me that rankles,' burst out Nora. 'Evelyn was so close, part of me, and I loved Danny – and they did that to *me*.'

'Want to tell me about it?' Baby had heard the story many times before, but it was polite to ask. There was so little else to talk about here. She never minded hearing it again. They all told and retold tales. You did here, somehow.

A simple story. Nora had trusted her friends Evelyn and Danny, and what had they done? They had asked her to collect a packet at the Post Office (despatched from Turkey) only for her to find the police there, ready waiting to pounce. Heroin. The hard stuff. She had suspected Danny of experimenting with cannabis, perhaps Evelyn, although she wasn't sure, but she herself had never touched anything.

It might be true, it might not, thought Baby, she kept an open mind. But telling it certainly made it seem true to Nora, and with this she sympathised.

'And a poet. I trusted Danny because he wrote poetry. Poetry ought to be trustworthy.' Baby understood that Nora had read English at her university: a Girton girl.

'Like Lord Tennyson, you mean? I suppose poetry has changed since his day.' No one had ever mentioned the names of Ezra Pound, or T. S. Eliot, or W. H. Auden, or Philip Larkin to Baby, but echoes from this wider world had somehow got through to her. Baby thought Nora such an innocent that her heart (usually so unyielding) quite melted towards her; she couldn't see her making a success of crime, the girl didn't seem able to distinguish between life and literature. Baby yawned. 'Was it potato pie for supper tonight?'

It was one of the ways of distinguishing the days. Potato pie was Wednesday.

'No. Lancashire hotpot and grease.'

Thursday then. One more day gone.

Baby got up from the bed and picked up the magazine she'd set aside to read on Friday; she saved up little treats for certain days as a means of making life bearable. But it was almost Friday, no sense in denying herself the small pleasure; Friday might never come. Although that was probably hoping too much. 'Got a fag?' She was a delicately boned, pretty woman, hungry now for life.

'No – Beryl?'

'Yes? Call me Baby, do. I prefer it to Beryl. Beryl sounds like a disease – "He died, covered with beryls and carbuncles". – Or else you could eat it. "Have a beryl on a pin, Winkle".' She must be drunk to talk like this. Perhaps the potato pie had fermented: that would make a powerful brew all right. Poteen, wasn't it?

'Baby, then,' said Nora. 'I think I'm going mad in here.'

'Me, too.'

'No, really.' Nora was quiet. 'When I looked in the mirror this morning, I didn't know my own face.'

'It's that mirror,' said Baby quickly, rather frightened, looking towards the cracked square stuck above the wash-basin. 'You wouldn't know your own mother in it.'

'That's just it – I thought it was my mother for a moment. I looked and first I saw a stranger's face, and then I thought, no – it's my mother. Then, click, I swear I heard a click, it was me. That was the worst moment of all.'

'Yes, I can see it might be.'

'Has it ever happened to you?'

Baby shook her head. Rotten as was the world and her own role in it, she was always firmly rooted in it. 'You'll be out soon. Not much longer for you.'

She reached out a hand to give Nora a sympathetic pat. She was surprised how much she felt for the girl. She not

125

only liked her, but she admired her educated intelligence. It was all such a *waste.*

'Yes. I'll miss you. You've been good to me.'

Nora had less than a month to go; Baby one month more. She had not been the most obliging and tractable of prisoners.

'I've liked our talks,' she said. 'All that stuff about books and pictures. No one ever talked like that to me before. I'd like to go and see some pictures some time,' said Baby wistfully. 'Say the National Gallery. You're not going to do the Gallery, are you?' Baby put her head on one side. 'That's not what you're going to hit?'

She got a small smile out of Nora. 'No . . . Thanks for what you said. But remember it works both ways. You taught me how to manage my hair.' She put up a hand to her long, dark hair, naturally straight, now slightly curled at the ends.

'As far as I could in here,' sighed Baby. In another meta-morphosis, Beryl Andrea Barker had been a hairdresser. 'The Governor was very good about the heated rollers when they blew up. It was because they were Spanish they fused the lights.' A certain holiday in Spain had not lived up to Baby's hopes (it was where Phil had left her), and so anything Spanish was wrong. It was her little obsession or madness. Everyone developed them in this place. 'Have you got anyone to go to when you get out, kid?'

'Mmm,' nodded Nora. 'More or less. What about you?'

'I've got a mate I can go to.' Bee Dawson, in fact, abandoned by the man she had hoped to marry, was as lonely as Baby, and had let her know she would be welcome. 'I'll give you the address.'

Nora nodded. 'Thanks, and you shall have mine. I don't know that I can complete your education, though, Baby.'

She went to the mirror and stared at herself for a longish time.

126

'See anyone nice?' asked Baby flippantly, to break the moment.

'No.'

The girl turned away, dropped to the floor, and started to crawl round on all fours.

Baby stared, then touched her. Nora was just not there at all. 'Lost something?' she said gaily. 'Hey, it's me, Baby.'

Nora hardly glanced at her. 'I'm looking for my pendant, the gold one. I must have lost it on the floor.'

'You haven't got a pendant.'

'Yes, I have. I always wear it. It has my name on it.'

'If you've got a pendant, Nora, then it's with all your own things that they take away, and you'll get it when you leave.' Unless someone's nicked it first, probably that could happen. Personally, she didn't trust the wardresses an inch. The police were all right, but the prison staff were ghastly. Except for the Governor. 'Come on, get up off your knees.'

She dragged the girl on to her own bed.

'There's nothing on the floor except the dirt and the odd mouse dropping, plenty of those.'

Privately, she thought the momentary lapse alarming. Perhaps Nora was going mad. But a request to see the doctor would only produce some Valium, and might retard her release. Do you get parole if you're bonkers?

In the event, it was Baby herself who went into the infirmary. Next day, as she walked down the staircase carrying a pile of trays, and thus unable to protect herself, someone gave her a hard shove, and she fell the whole flight, landing on the concrete floor below to receive mild concussion and a broken leg.

It was impossible to discover who had pushed her, but Baby herself thought it was probably the woman whose hair she had burned when the Spanish hair-rollers over-heated and blew up. The matter was never cleared up. She

127

was just another unsolved crime statistic, and in prison, too. She had no idea, of course, that she was going to be any thing more than that.

When she returned to her cell (she avoided the name as much as possible, preferring room, or even "place", but sometimes its reality was unavoidable), Nora was gone, and her companion now was, as luck would have it (or the deliberate nastiness of that red-haired wardress), the lady with the singed hair. They were both glad to see the last of each other, when Baby's time was up.

She was still limping when she left prison. Bee met her in the car.

'You *were* unlucky,' said Bee. 'You should have paid the fine instead of going to prison. I'm sure you could have done.'

'I hadn't got it. Phil made off with every last penny we had.'

Bee drew in her breath sharply. She felt strongly about money. A page of accounts was a poem to her.

'We've both been let down. I expected to be married by now. Fancy Phil doing that. I thought she depended on you. Absolutely depended. We all said so. Baby's the strong one, we said.'

'The love and affection I poured out on that woman. I'm a naturally maternal type. Wasted. She said she could not stand my voice.'

'With me it was my hair – he said it smelt. My psychiatrist says men often present reasons like that, when they want out. There's always something. All fantasy, of course.' It was not surprising to Beryl that her friend had a psychiatrist, because she believed in professionals. If Bee had troubles, she wanted them sorted out by a trained hand, and a bill presented. When she had the bill receipted and filed she would be cured. 'He says most men

128

have a split personality: it's the extra chromosome for maleness, he reckons.'

Bee had further advice to offer.

'I think you ought to drop the Baby and call yourself Beryl,' she suggested. 'My psychiatrist is against pet names. Belittling, he says. You're a big girl now.'

'I'll try,' agreed Beryl Andrea Barker. 'Hell, you're right. What if it does sound like a vitamin deficiency: beryl-beryl. I owe it to myself.'

Beryl waited patiently for Nora to get in touch with her. 'Nora knows where to find me,' she assured herself, 'because I told her. Saw her write it down. So, although I can't get in touch with her, she can get in touch with me.'

She was confident she would hear, because there really had been a bond between them, not strong but growing, and it was in the nature of an educational tie: she wanted to learn and Nora wanted to teach. Nora was a natural teacher and this had probably been her profession, although she had never said so directly. But Beryl had got the distinct impression that the terrible Evelyn was a very different sort from Nora.

Nora was, indeed, just the kind of young woman to be taken advantage of by the unscrupulous, that was clear, but Beryl believed that she was unlikely to fall into Evelyn's clutches again. 'I shan't link up with her any more,' Nora had stated. But her friend knew well that there were only too many Evelyns, and Dannys too, in this world, and that they would always find Nora out. Beryl's anxieties were aroused.

The weeks passed. Beryl bought herself two new wigs (prison food was death to the hair), one ash-blonde, one red-gold, and launched herself into life. No letters and no telephone calls came for Beryl Andrea Barker from Nora. Beryl and Bee were living in a London suburb, having pre-ferred not to go back to the southern town where they had lived before, although Baby (she relapsed occasionally into being Baby), kept up an odd, intermittent relationship with the policewoman who had investigated the crimes for which their group, Diana, Bee, Phil and Baby, had been responsible, and for which only Bee had suffered imprisonment. Diana had died too soon for that sort of punishment. Both Beryl and Bee were now in work.

Beryl did not give up the quest for Nora without a struggle. She made cautious enquiries through the chaplain at the prison. He told her that Nora was now out of parole, and free of all checks. He had no address.

'He doesn't want you to have it,' said Bee. 'Natural. Divide and rule. That's how they operate.'

'You may be right,' said Beryl, uneasily. What she really thought was that Nora had disappeared on purpose. She was planning something.

Revenge, it had to be revenge against Danny and Evelyn. Knowing what she did about Nora's state of mind, it looked obvious.

'Maybe I ought to warn them?'

'How?' said Bee. 'You don't have an address, and you only know their Christian names. Let them be. They've got it coming to them.'

'It's Nora I'm thinking of,' admitted Beryl.

After Christmas, with no card, no present, nothing (and she *had* hoped, and had a bottle of *Arpège* ready gift-wrapped for Nora), she took action.

She sent a letter addressed to Nora at her old Cambridge college and marked the envelope "Please Forward: Urgent", and underlined "Urgent".

In about a week the letter came back with an accompanying note saying that no one of this name was, or ever had been, connected with the College.

Beryl received the letter sadly. She was only glad that she had not told Bee, because Bee would have said One

More Lie. But Beryl knew it was not precisely a lie: somehow, somewhere, it was a truth.

She was beginning to be afraid that it was already too late to help the girl. Every day she studied the newspapers for reports of violence offered towards anyone called Dan or Danny or Evelyn. Nothing appeared.

Her leg was mending nicely and she no longer used a stick, but the doctor said she might always limp a bit when tired. The muscle needed strengthening; he suggested swimming.

Baby (she felt like Baby) bought a new bikini (her old one having been bleached by the strong Spanish sun), embroidered her initials BAB on the leg, and practised total immersion. She went every Wednesday. Bee lent her the car, so she drove; she had learnt to drive in Spain and it showed.

Two Wednesdays passed, and although the leg improved, her driving did not. She was driving slowly and nervously down the road from the swimming-pool, trying to remember whether you stopped at a flashing-light or drove straight through, when she saw a young woman about to cross the road.

Without meaning to, she pressed on the accelerator and the car shot forward. The young woman gave her a scared glance and leapt for the pavement.

But Beryl had seen her face clearly. It was because she had seen her face that her foot had slipped. 'Nora – and I nearly ran her down.'

Beryl saw Nora and Nora saw Beryl. Nora ran. Or did she?

Beryl stopped the car, and got out. But Nora had already disappeared from sight.

Sick with disappointment, she went back to the car and sat hunched over the wheel.

'It was her, though. She was wearing a head scarf, a

glint of something gold round her neck, red earrings, but I'd know her face anywhere. I couldn't be mistaken.'

Puzzled, she drove home. 'I suppose she didn't see me. Well, she *did,* but she didn't know it was me.'

'So she hasn't killed anyone yet, then,' said Bee, when she was told.

'She's getting close to it, though.'

'So you've got telepathy? How can you possibly know that?'

'I saw her face, remember. I saw her expression.'

'You'd just scared her to death.'

'She wasn't scared,' said Beryl. 'Not her.'

Not her. Me, Beryl thought. I was frightened by what I saw in her face. A wildness that was never there before.

'Let's tell the tea leaves,' said Bee. 'I never used to believe in them, but I do now. I've changed.' She swirled her cup. 'There, look – a monster, a two-headed monster. That's you.'

'Thanks.'

'Well, it must be: two wigs and there's me – spectacles, you can see them, can't you?' She held the cup sideways. 'Can't see your friend?' There was slight malice in her tone.

'Someone came to see you today while you were out,' she added slyly. Bee worked shifts, so she was often home when Beryl wasn't. It was a strange limbo-world they lived in.

'Who? – Nora?'

'Couldn't really see – Gone before I could get to the door – Looked like a policeman to me, from the back.'

'What?'

'Yes. What have you been up to?'

'Nothing. Of course, he wasn't a policeman. Probably the gasman. Or a canvasser, or one of these people making surveys.' Nerves made her voice sharp.

132

'If he was a policemen he will be back,' said Bee, with unanswerable logic.

He came back the next night, when fortunately Bee was out, to ask her if she knew the whereabouts of Nora Underwood.

'No,' said Beryl in alarm. 'Why?'

'You were enquiring about her, though?'

'But doesn't that just show I don't know where she is?' What a magnificent display of police backward-looking logic, she thought, and goodness knew what duplicity it masked. Double talk, just to get her to incriminate herself.

'She has been sending threatening letters to a Mr Daniel Blakeheart. It would really be in her own best interests if she stopped. He says he won't take any action if she promises to leave him alone.'

'I don't know where she is,' said Beryl.

He looked round the room. 'She gave this address. Wrote from here.'

'I haven't seen her for weeks,' shouted Beryl. She limped to the door, almost needing a stick, she felt so sick and weak. 'Please go away, and believe me I don't know where she is.'

He did go, reluctantly, looking as if he might be back. 'Do you live here alone?' he asked.

'I've got a flat-mate,' she said. 'She works shifts.'

'Back this evening?'

'Probably,' said Beryl, not liking what she heard in his voice.

Thanking her lucky stars that Bee was not at home, Beryl searched the whole flat from top to bottom, but, of course, Nora was *not* there, and no sign that she ever had been or ever would be. How could it be otherwise?

The policeman was back that evening, accompanied by a woman police constable. Bee was present too, an explosive situation in itself. Beryl knew there would be upbraiding and a scene afterwards. Pity she didn't see the policeman's visit in the tea leaves, she thought, or she might have stayed out this evening.

But it wasn't until the policeman, using the police-woman and Bee as witnesses, asked her to copy out a few phrases of ill-wishes to one Danny Blakeheart, that Beryl realised the police suspected *her* of writing the letters. In her agitation she wrote Blakeheart as Blackheart, which was certainly how she felt, but no indication of her innocence.

She saw the policeman smile at this, and point it out to his colleague, who remained straight-faced. Beryl had the horrible feeling that life was packing her up in a parcel and posting her somewhere nasty.

'Oh, Nora, Nora, you would not do this to me?' She apostrophised the absent Nora.

Her desire to find Nora was strengthened now by the threat to herself.

'I wish they'd let me see the envelope, so I had this Danny's address,' she complained to Bee. 'Then I might track down Nora. She must be, well, watching him, if she means to attack him, and I could watch the house for *her*.'

'Then you *would* be in trouble. Don't you suppose the police aren't watching too? Probably arrest you at once. I don't know what's coming over you. You used not to be violent.'

'I'm not violent,' protested Beryl.

'They say you cut some woman's hair off in prison.'

'I didn't cut it: it fell off.'

'I don't understand you, Beryl Andrea Barker. Why don't you forget all this business? Forget this Nora?' Beryl shook her head.

'I want to warn her and stop her. Revenge isn't worth it.'

'That isn't what I've heard you say in the past.'

'It's what I say now.'

Bee looked perplexed. 'I don't know why you're so concerned about her.'

Because she represented a bit of civilisation at a time when my life was dirty and ugly; because she opened a door for me to a world that I didn't know existed; because we were mates, at a bad time for us both, and I owe her for that.

In a worried voice, Bee said, 'You know, to make the police investigate in that way, in depth, as you might say, there has to have been more than just one letter. She has to have done more than that. You don't really know what sort of a record she's got.'

'I know what she did her time for,' said Beryl shortly. 'No secrets in there, I can tell you.'

'But you don't know her past. What she's been up to before.'

'Up to.' Beryl could hardly hear that phrase in connection with the dignified, if sometimes reserved young woman she had known.

'Your leg's aching,' said Bee sympathetically. 'Go to bed and I'll get you a hottie. Whisky?'

Beryl went swimming three times that week, and each time she drove home very slowly, window wound down, hugging the kerb and studying the faces of the passers-by, hoping to see Nora near where she had seen her before.

It was raining again on the third night, and the gutters were full of puddles. At one corner she saw a police car parked. She could see the driver was watching. 'Here I am kerb-crawling,' she groaned to herself. 'Probably get arrested for that next!'

At that moment she saw a slim figure wearing a raincoat, with her hair loose on her shoulders. She was striding along, head up.

'Nora, Nora,' she called. 'It's me, Baby.'

Nora swung round, a big smile crossed her face, and she called out, 'Oh, how lovely to see you. Oh, I am glad. I thought we'd never see each other again, and I *did* so want to. How lovely.'

All over me, thought Beryl. Well, I'm blowed.

Nora got in the car, and Beryl drove off, hardly knowing where she was going, just driving on. She was wondering what to do for the best.

Out of the corner of her eye, she studied Nora. Except for the fact that she'd lost weight and was a better colour, she looked as Beryl remembered her, sober, reliable and gentle. The wild look was gone.

No gold pendant around her neck today; she wasn't wearing one. No red earrings, either. Everyone has their different outfits for different days, thought Beryl. I do myself. It's a mood thing.

'Why didn't you write?'

'Why didn't you?' demanded Nora.

'I didn't have your address.'

'I'm sure I gave it to you.'

'No,' and Beryl was sure she hadn't. 'I broke my leg, remember. But you had mine.'

'No, I didn't,' said Nora.

A silent shriek rose inside Beryl, you did, you did, you used it to write a threatening letter to Danny. She swallowed the words.

'You wrote it down,' she said gently. 'On a card.' She could understand that the girl wouldn't want to admit the use she'd made of it. Later, she'd have to explain, but play it quietly for now.

Nora was silent. She seemed unable to say more about the address, but she looked thoughtful.

Apparently taking on a life of its own, the car was heading into central London. It wasn't exactly out of Beryl's control, but she had the sense of doing as the

136

machine directed. Automatic transmission, she giggled. I'm hysterical, that's what, hysteria rages.

'Friend?' she said, reaching out a hand towards Nora. 'I mean, there were some good moments in that place, weren't there? There were for me.'

They continued talking for a few minutes before Nora said, 'We'll be in Trafalgar Square soon. You'll have to turn round and drive back. I've got to go to work.'

'What work do you do?' A roundabout appeared, opportunely, so that Beryl could circle back on her tracks.

'Oh, in a hospital. Night duty.'

'As a nurse?'

'No, clerical work. Nothing important. All I could get. You know how it is.'

'You live near where I found you walking?' It had not escaped Beryl that no address was forthcoming.

'Some distance away,' said Nora evasively.

'I saw you the other night. Three nights ago – nearly ran you over.'

'Oh –' Nora sounded vague. 'Do you know, I don't remember.'

'No, you didn't see me. But I saw you. Noticed you'd found your gold pendant.' She couldn't resist the comment.

Nora shook her head. 'I haven't got a gold pendant.' Then she added thoughtfully, 'As a matter of fact, I was in bed with a migraine that night. I remember now.'

'All right, then. You haven't got a pendant, and you weren't there that night, and I didn't nearly run you over. Two other people.'

The car skidded to a stop around a quiet corner.

'You can get out here.'

Nora scrambled out and stood there, looking lost. 'I don't know why you're so angry.'

'Because I like a bit of straightforwardness and truth occasionally.' And Beryl started to drive away.

Nora ran after the car and banged on the window.

'Well, what is it?'

'Just give me a lift to the hospital where I work. Please.'

Silently Beryl opened the car door. 'Get in.'

She let the girl direct her through the streets to the hospital: the St Aloysius General Hospital. She stopped the car and then sat there looking at her.

'And if I go in there and ask for you, what name will you be using?' she asked sardonically. 'Or will they say they've never heard of you before?'

'Ah, don't be like that. You never used to be.'

'We were equal in prison. Mates, level with each other. Or at least I thought we were.'

Nora got out of the car. 'There's not much chance for us to meet, with you working all day and me at night, but there's Saturday and Sunday. Meet me at twelve o'clock on Saturday at the National Gallery. On the steps.'

'Before I come, tell me this much: have you ever killed anyone? No. Are you planning to kill someone? All right, don't answer. But let me just tell you this: I nearly killed someone once, a woman, and I know what it feels like. Don't go down that alley unless you're very sure. It's not nice.'

And, for once, feeling she had said something true and real, Beryl Andrea Barker drove away.

She was not sure if she'd keep the appointment on Saturday. She might or she might not.

In the days before the weekend, the weather worsened. Rain and high winds made life unpleasant.

On the Friday, Beryl saw a short news item in the evening paper about a young man being attacked by a girl with a knife; the girl escaped. Beryl did not show it to Bee, and although she applied her own critical faculty to it, telling herself that no name was given, yet she was convinced that the man was Danny and the woman with the knife was Nora.

Finally she telephoned the hospital and asked to speak to Nora.

She got the reply that Nora hadn't been at work for a week.

At least she worked there, thought Beryl, and used the name I knew. She was grateful for that piece of truth.

The hospital had no address, though. Nora had told them she was moving her lodging. And that was probably true also, thought Beryl sourly.

On the Saturday she kept her appointment with Nora at the National Gallery. Not with a great deal of hope, but she went.

Twelve o'clock came, so did twelve-fifteen.

At twelve-thirty she looked out from the balcony, and saw Nora threading her way through the traffic of Trafalgar Square. Slowly she walked up the steps, not seeming to see Beryl, but moving steadily towards her.

'You're late.'

'I know,' said Nora. 'The traffic's so heavy. I knew you'd wait. Let's go and look at the pictures.'

She was wearing a loose raincoat and scarf, with a big bag over her arm.

'Before we do, tell me why you offer so many lies.'

Nora looked surprised. 'Everything I say is true.'

'No, it isn't. For instance, you weren't held up by the traffic. You were standing across the road in Trafalgar Square, your face turned this way for quite half an hour. I saw you.'

'I was watching for someone,' admitted Nora.

'And?'

'She didn't come. I think someone else did, though,' Nora ended thoughtfully.

'You mean Danny and Evelyn? It's them you are talking about?'

Nora bowed her head. 'I don't think she came.'

'You don't seem very clear,' said Beryl, remorselessly. 'Are you going to kill them, Nora? Is that what you got me here for? As a sort of witness.'

'I think *they'd* like to kill *me*.'

'Oh rubbish.' Beryl was angry.

The rain had stopped, but the clouds were lower than ever, the air oppressively warm for the season. A flash of lightning cracked across the sky, followed by a roll of thunder. A group of people standing under the portico were lit up dramatically, Beryl and Nora among them.

Nora dropped her bag, some of the contents spilling out. Beryl helped retrieve various objects, among which was a gold pendant. She handed it over to Nora without a word.

'I don't remember that,' said Nora.

'Or do you? Don't let's get into that again.' She noticed that Nora was trembling, and a vivid colour was rising in her cheeks. The thunder, or something else, had excited her. Fear didn't seem to be quite the word. There was too much energy involved: fear is quieter. 'Let's get inside.'

They entered the gallery, glad to be out of the storm. Without meaning it to happen, they found they were absorbed into a group of people being taken round the gallery by a woman guide.

In this manner they entered a room devoted to French paintings of the eighteenth century. They seemed to have no message to convey to Beryl, other than an impression that French agriculture then had been in a bad way and a revolution understandable.

'We are really too large a group to go round in comfort,' pronounced their guide. 'Separate into two groups and go round in opposite directions.'

She took a firm grip of Beryl's elbow and moved her on. Nora was in the other group, untethered but unresistant.

'Meet in the entrance hall in ten minutes,' hissed Beryl

to Nora. Not sorry to be shot of me, she thought.

She was there herself in nine minutes. No Nora.

'None expected,' she said to herself, but gave the girl the one minute more. Then she set off, going anti-clockwise through the rooms she had just left behind her.

There were the two groups still walking round and very nearly on the point of meeting each other.

Nora wasn't among them.

Beryl realised that a young man was also making a circuit of the rooms: clockwise to her contrary motion. Presently they both ended up in the entrance foyer.

He was a tall, fair-haired young man wearing jeans and a loose jacket. He looked cold and miserable. There might or might not be the creamy-white of bandage showing at the unbuttoned neck of his shirt, Beryl couldn't be sure. What she was sure of, so unexpectedly, was that, although he was young and tense, and might certainly be silly, he was not wicked.

If that was Danny, he was a babe in the wood as much as Nora.

Soberly, she went over and spoke. 'I got the idea you were looking for someone just now. Is she dark haired, wearing a tweed coat?'

Stiffly (it was true then, he *did* have a chest wound and it made speech difficult), he said 'I would not call her dark – more fair. I'm not an expert on girls' hair. We arranged to meet here.'

'You know the difference between fair and dark, don't you?' said Beryl sharply. 'Wait here, and watch out.' For yourself as well as her, she thought. She hurried towards the Ladies' Cloakroom.

In the washroom there was nobody but a stout woman replenishing the paper towels.

'Did you see a fair young woman come in here? Or a dark one? Or both of them together.'

'I shouldn't notice, dear. If they had two heads each, I doubt if I'd notice. They come in and they go out.' She shrugged. 'I did see one young woman fiddling with her face and she left this lipstick behind.' She handed it to Beryl. Bright red lipstick, Evelyn-red, not Nora-pink. 'If you know her you can give it to her.'

Beryl took it. 'Not me, but I think I know someone who does.'

She hurried back to where she had left Danny, but he had gone.

From the entrance she just made out his figure, disappearing across Trafalgar Square towards the tube station.

Out of her pocket she drew a card which had fallen from Nora's bag when she dropped it. On it was an address, which was why Beryl had appropriated it.

Although the address was in an area not far away, and one which she had got to know, Beryl got lost twice, before finding her way to the house in question.

When she saw a telephone box on the corner of the road, she took one precaution: she telephoned Bee. 'I'm going to No 12 Ashley Road.' From where she stood she could see the house, a three-storey affair of greying yellow brick. 'I must go – she had a knife in her bag. I saw it gleam. There'll be murder done. I thought she might kill even me.'

'You're mad,' said Bee.

'If I go down, tell that woman detective who put us away, Charmian Daniels. I feel I owe it to her.'

'What does that mean?' asked Bee, but she asked it of silence: Beryl was gone.

As soon as Beryl stepped inside No 12, she knew it was the sort of place where you could be murdered to music without anyone taking any notice at all, except to turn the television up higher. The stairs smelt of damp and mice,

142

together with something deeper and darker, but definitely human.

A row of pigeon holes with names showed her that Flat Five, Top Floor, was lived in by D. Blakeheart, and on the same card a second name had been pencilled underneath his name. It looked like E. Ash, but someone had scored it through, quite nastily, with something sharp.

So they were living together? Of course. Oh, how unwise. Silly young man. What has he let himself in for? Did he understand what was up? But I didn't myself till the National Gallery.

She laboured up the stairs, it was like climbing Everest, her legs felt so heavy and her breath was so short. Perhaps the air was getting thinner? And was the alarm that filled her mind the fantasy of an oxygen-starved brain?

'Loony,' she said to herself. 'You'd never heard of oxygen starvation till you met Nora.'

On the top floor the house narrowed to two rooms facing each other across a narrow landing. Both doors stood open, one very wide.

Beryl stood on the threshold. She didn't need to go in to read the story. On every side were the signs of destruction, as if a battle for survival had raged here.

A blonde wig had been wrenched into pieces, while individual yellow curls had been torn off and splattered about the room. Face powder had been emptied on the bed and a bottle of scent cracked against the wall. A musky, sweet smell hung over everything.

On the dressing-table mirror a lipstick had been used to scrawl a message. *You're dead, sweet cow.*

Beryl read it and understood. 'That's the end of the road for Evelyn, she's been killed.'

She pushed open the door to the next room. A body lying against it meant she had to push hard to get in. She could see the legs as she shoved at the door.

Danny was lying on his back, face towards the ceiling, eyes half-open. He must be dead. A knife protruded at an angle from his chest, it looked ludicrous, absurd, obscene, like an ornament, strangely worn. There was blood everywhere.

In one corner crouched Nora. She was looking at her, Beryl.

'Did you do this, Nora? Kill Danny?'

The girl shook her head. 'No, no. Nora didn't do it. She's gone now; she was unstable, poor thing. Better without her. The same with Evelyn, silly girl, got us all into trouble. I think it was *her* that killed Danny. I shall see she gets the blame. The guilt is hers.'

'Oh Nora,' said Beryl, before she could stop herself. But who was she talking to?

In a bright, cheerful voice, the girl announced: 'Oh no, I'm not Nora. I'm Maureen.'

There was shouting from below and then feet pounding up the stairs. A tall West Indian came into the room.

'That's blood coming through my ceiling. Where's it coming from?'

He saw Danny and knelt beside him.

'He's dead, I think,' said Beryl.

'No, he's not dead.' The man spoke with the assurance of one used to knife wounds. 'But he will be soon if he doesn't get to hospital. What the hell's going on up here?' He looked at Nora. 'She used to live here once – but lately she's only seemed to stand outside a lot. Saw her today.'

In a soft voice the girl crouched in the corner spoke.

'Once there was a girl called Margaret, who went to Cambridge, but she couldn't cope, so a girl called Nora was born, but she couldn't keep the girl called Evelyn out of trouble, so Maureen has come and *she* can cope.'

Once there was a girl called Margaret who went to

144

Cambridge as a student, but it was all too much for her and she had a breakdown, and a girl called Nora emerged, looking for a fresh start; but she brought along with her Evelyn who was everything Nora was not, flashy, blonde, and highly sexed. Nora knew a bit about Evelyn, but not much, while Evelyn only knew Nora got in her way when Danny and fun were about. Danny knew both Nora and Evelyn, but thought they were just one girl with moods, while *they* knew they were not. He was the sort of person who used several names himself, quite in the way of business, so it never surprised him that Nora-Evelyn did it too. But the three of them made an explosive bundle with a guilt and hate distributed unequally among them: Nora hated both Danny and Evelyn, while Evelyn only hated Nora, and Danny hated no one.

'I think it was the thunderstorm and that flash of lightning that forced the issue,' said Beryl to Bee. 'I think she looked in her mirror when she dropped her bag, and saw that face that looked like her mother's and *that's* when Maureen came in. Otherwise I think Evelyn would have met Danny after Nora had finished with me. But she was in a bad mood, anyway. I saw her when she was watching from across Trafalgar Square. Do you understand me?'

'Just about,' said Bee. 'Still, smart detective work from you.'

So the time in prison which turned Nora into a criminal, turned Beryl into a detective, and for a moment she was pleased and wondered if *this* was her new life to be. Then she remembered how she had liked the girl, and wanted to help her, and she was sad.

'I wonder if she'll get better?'

'Difficult cases, these multiple-split personalities,' said Bee. Her psychiatrist had said so.

Beryl sighed, conscious of all the unborn, warring selves inside her head, and went to the cupboard where she kept her wigs, and locked it.

Tomorrow she'd sell them. No sense in encouraging three heads to grow where one would do.

Ellis Peters

EYE WITNESS

———————————————————————————————

It was undoubtedly inconsiderate of Brother Ambrose to fall ill with a raging quinsy just a few days before the yearly rents were due for collection, and leave the rolls still uncopied, and the new entries still to be made. No one knew the abbey rolls as Brother Ambrose did. He had been clerk to Brother Matthew, the cellarer, for four years, during which time fresh grants to the abbey had been flooding in richly, a new mill on the Tern, pastures, assarts, messuages in the town, glebes in the countryside, a fishery up-river, even a church or two, and there was no one who could match him at putting a finger on the slip-pery tenant or the field-lawyer, or the householder who had always three good stories to account for his inability to pay. And here was the collection only a day away, and Brother Ambrose on his back in the infirmary, croaking like a sick raven, and about as much use.

Brother Matthew's chief steward, who always made the collection within the town and suburbs of Shrewsbury in person, took it almost as a personal injury. He had had to install as substitute a young lay clerk who had entered the abbey service not four months previously. Not that he had found any cause to complain of the young man's work. He had copied industriously and neatly, and shown great alertness and interest in his quick grasp of what he copied,

147

making round, respectful eyes at the value of the rent-roll.

But Master William Rede had been put out, and was bent on letting everyone know of it. He was a querulous, argumentative man in his fifties, who, if you said white to him, would inevitably say black, and bring documentary evidence to back up his contention. He came to visit his old friend and helper in the abbey infirmary, the day before the town collection was due, but whether to comfort or reproach was matter for speculation. Brother Ambrose, still voiceless, essayed speech and achieved only a painful wheeze, before Brother Cadfael, who was anointing his patient's throat afresh with goose-grease, and had a soothing syrup of orpine standing by, laid a palm over the sufferer's mouth and ordered silence.

'Now, William,' he said tolerantly, 'if you can't comfort, don't vex. This poor soul's got you on his conscience as it is, and you know, as well as I do, that you have the whole matter at your finger-ends. You tell him so, and fetch up a smile, or out you go.' And he wrapped a length of good Welsh flannel round the glistening throat, and reached for the spoon that stood in the beaker of syrup. Brother Ambrose opened his mouth with the devoted resignation of a little bird waiting to be fed, and sucked in the dose with an expression of slightly surprised appreciation.

But William Rede was not going to be done out of his grievance so easily. 'Oh, no fault of yours,' he owned grudgingly, 'but very ill luck for me, as if I had not enough on my hands in any event, with the rent-roll grown so long, and the burden of scribe's work for ever lengthening, as it does. And I have troubles of my own nearer home, into the bargain, with that rogue son of mine nothing but brawler and gamester as he is. If I've told him once I've told him a score of times, the next time he comes to me to pay his debts or buy him out of trouble, he'll come in vain, he may sweat it out in gaol, and serve him

148

right. A man would think he could get a little peace and comfort from his own flesh and blood. All I get is vexation.'

Once launched upon this tune, he was liable to continue the song indefinitely, and Brother Ambrose was already looking apologetic and abject, as though not William, but he, had engendered the unsatisfactory son. Cadfael could not recall that he had ever spoken with young Rede, beyond exchanging the time of day, and knew enough about fathers and sons, and the expectations each had of the other, to take all such complaints with wary reserve. Report certainly said the young man was a wild one, but at twenty-two which of the town hopefuls was not? By thirty they were most of them working hard, and minding their own purses, homes and wives.

'Your lad will mend, like many another,' said Cadfael comfortably, edging the voluble visitor out from the infirmary into the sunshine of the great court. Before them on their left the great west tower of the church loomed; on their right, the long block of the guest-halls, and beyond, the crowns of the garden trees just bursting into leaf and bud, with a moist, pearly light filming over stonework and cobbles and all with a soft Spring sheen. 'And as for the rents, you know very well, old humbug, that you have your finger on every line of the leiger book, and tomorrow's affair will go like a morning walk. At any rate, you can't complain of your prentice hand. He's worked hard enough over those books of yours.'

'Jacob has certainly shown application,' the steward agreed cautiously. 'I own I've been surprised at the grasp he has of abbey affairs, in so short a time. Young people nowadays take so little interest in what they're set to do – fly-by-nights and frivolous, most of them. It's been heartening to see one of them work with such zeal. I dare-

149

say he knows the value due from every property of the house by this time. Yes, a good boy. But too ingenuous, Cadfael, there's his flaw – too affable. Figures and characters on vellum cannot baffle him, but a rogue with a friendly tongue might come over him. He cannot stand men off – he cannot put frost between. It's not well to be too open with all men.'

It was mid-afternoon; in an hour or so it would be time for Vespers. The great court had always some steady flow of activity, but at this hour it was at its quietest. They crossed the court together at leisure, Brother Cadfael to return to his workshop in the herb garden, the steward to the north walk of the cloister, where his assistant was hard at work in the scriptorium. But before they had reached the spot where their paths would divide, two young men emerged from the cloister in easy conversation, and came towards them.

Jacob of Bouldon was a sturdy, square-set young fellow from the south of the shire, with a round, amiable face, large, candid eyes, and a ready smile. He came with a vellum leaf doubled in one hand, and a pen behind his ear, in every particular the eager, hard-working clerk. A little too open to any man's approaches, perhaps, as his master had said? The lanky, narrow-headed fellow attentive at his side had a very different look about him, weather-beaten, sharp-eyed and drab in hard-wearing dark clothes, with a leather jerkin to bear the rubbing of a heavy pack. The back of the left shoulder was scrubbed pallid and dull from much carrying, and his hat was wide and drooping of brim, to shed off rain. A travelling haber-dasher with a few days' business in Shrewsbury, no novelty in the commoners' guest-hall of the abbey. His like were always on the roads, somewhere about the shire.

The pedlar louted to Master William with obsequious respect, said his goodday, and made off to his lodging.

Early to be home for the night, surely, but perhaps he had done good business and come back to replenish his stock. A wise tradesman kept something in reserve, when he had a safe store to hand, rather than carry his all on every foray.

Master William looked after him with no great favour. 'What had that fellow to do thus with you, boy?' he questioned suspiciously. 'He's a deal too curious, with that long nose of his. I've seen him making up to any of the household he can back into a corner. What was he after in the scriptorium?'

Jacob opened his wide eyes even wider. 'Oh, he's an honest fellow enough, sir, I'm sure. Though he does like to probe into everything, I grant you, and asks a lot of questions . . .'

'Then you give him no answers,' said the steward firmly.

'I don't, nothing but general talk that leaves him no wiser. Though I think he's but naturally inquisitive and no harm meant. He likes to curry favour with everyone, but that's by way of his trade. A rough-tongued pedlar would not sell many tapes and laces,' said the young man blithely, and flourished the leaf of vellum he carried. 'I was coming to ask you about this carucate of land in Recordine – there's an erasure in the leiger book, I looked up the copy to compare. You'll remember, sir, it was disputed land for a while, the heir tried to recover it . . .'

'I do recall. Come, I'll show you the original copy. But have as little to say to these travelling folk as you can with civility,' Master William adjured earnestly. 'There are rogues on the roads as well as honest tradesmen. There, you go before, I'll follow you.'

He looked after the jaunty figure as it departed smartly, back to the scriptorium. 'As I said, Cadfael, too easily pleased with every man. It's not wise to look always for the best in men. But for all that,' he added, reverting morosely to his private grievance, 'I wish that scamp of mine was more like him. In debt already for some gambling folly, and he has to get himself picked up by the sergeants for a street brawl, and fined, and cannot pay the fine. And to keep my own name in respect, he's confident I shall have to buy him clear. I must see to it tomorrow, one way or the other, when I've finished my rounds in the town, for he has but three days left to pay. If it weren't for his mother . . . Even so, even so, this time I ought to let him stew.'

He departed after his clerk, shaking his head bitterly over his troubles. And Cadfael went off to see what feats of idiocy or genius Brother Oswin had wrought in the herb garden in his absence.

In the morning, when the brothers came out from Prime, Brother Cadfael saw the steward departing to begin his round, the deep leather satchel secured to his locked belt, and swinging by two stout straps. By evening it would be heavy with the annual wealth of the city rents, and those from the northern suburbs outside the walls. Jacob was there to see him go, listening dutifully to his last emphatic instructions, and sighing as he was left behind to complete the book-work. Warin Harefoot, the packman, was off early, too, to ply his trade among the housewives either of the town or the parish of the Foregate. A pliable fellow, full of professional bows and smiles, but by the look of him all his efforts brought him no better than a meagre living.

So there went Jacob, back to his pen and inkhorn in the cloisters, and forth to his important business went Master William. And who knows, thought Cadfael, which is in the right, the young man who sees the best in all, and trusts all, or the old one who suspects all until he has probed them through and through? The one may stumble into a snare now and then, but at least enjoy sunshine along the way, between falls. The other may never miss his footing, but seldom experience joy. Better find a way somewhere between!

It was a curious chance that seated him next to Brother Eutropius at breakfast, for what did anyone know about Brother Eutropius? He had come to the abbey of Saint Peter and Saint Paul of Shrewsbury only two months ago, from a minor grange of the order. But in two months of Brother Oswin, say, that young man would have been an open book to every reader, whereas Eutropius contained himself as tightly as did his skin, and gave out much less in the way of information. A taciturn man, thirty or so at a guess, who kept himself apart and looked solitary discontent at everything that crossed his path, but never complained. It might be merely newness and shyness, in one naturally uncommunicative, or it might be a gnawing inward anger against his lot and all the world. Rumour said, a man frustrated in love, and finding no relief in his resort to the cowl. But rumour was using its imagination, for want of fuel more reliable.

Eutropius also worked under Brother Matthew, the cellarer, and was intelligent and literate, but not a good or a quick scribe. Perhaps, when Brother Ambrose fell ill, he would have liked to be trusted to take over his books. Perhaps he resented the lay clerk being preferred before him. Perhaps! With Eutropius everything, thus far, was conjecture. Some day someone would pierce that carapace of his, with an unguarded word or a sudden irresistible motion of grace, and the mystery would no longer be a mystery, or the stranger a stranger.

Brother Cadfael knew better than to be in a hurry, where souls were concerned. There was plenty of elbow-room in eternity.

In the afternoon, returning to the grange court to collect

some seed he had left stored in the loft, Cadfael encountered Jacob, his scribing done for the moment, setting forth importantly with his own leather satchel into the Foregate.

'So he's left you a parcel to clear for him,' said Cadfael.

'I would gladly have done more,' said Jacob, mildly aggrieved and on his dignity. He looked less than his twenty-five years, well-grown as he was, with that cherubic face. 'But he says I'm sure to be slow, not knowing the rounds or the tenants, so he's let me take only the outlying lanes here in the Foregate, where I can take my time. I daresay he's right, it will take me longer than I think. I'm sorry to see him so worried about his son,' he said, shaking his head. 'He has to see to this business with the law, he told me not to worry if he was late returning today. I hope all goes well,' said the loyal subordinate, and set forth sturdily to do his own duty towards his master, however beset he might be by other cares.

Cadfael took his seed back to the garden, put in an hour or so of contented work there, washed his hands, and went to check on the progress of Brother Ambrose, who was just able to croak in his ear, more audibly than yesterday: 'I could rise and help poor William – such a day for him . . .'

He was halted there by a large, rough palm. 'Lie quiet,' said Cadfael, 'like a wise man. Let them see how well they can fend without you, and they'll value you the better hereafter. And about time, too!' And he fed his captive bird again, and returned to his labours in the garden.

At Vespers, Brother Eutropius came late and in haste, and took his place breathing rapidly, but as impenetrable as ever. And when they emerged to go to supper in the refectory, Jacob of Bouldon was just coming in at the gatehouse with his leather satchel of rents jealously guarded by one hand and looking round hopefully for his master, who had not yet returned. Nor had he some twenty minutes later, when supper was over; but in the gathering dusk Warin Harefoot trudged wearily across the court to the guest-hall, and the pack on his shoulder looked hardly lighter than when he had gone out in the morning.

Madog of the Dead-Boat, in addition to his primary means of livelihood, which was salvaging dead bodies from the River Severn at any season, had a number of seasonal occupations that afforded him sport as well as a living. Of these the one he enjoyed most was fishing, and of all the fishing seasons the one he liked best was the early Spring run up-river of the mature salmon, fine, energetic young males which had arrived early in the estuary, and would run and leap like athletes many miles upstream before they spawned. Madog was expert at taking them, and had had one out of the water this same day, before he paddled his coracle into the thick bushes under the castle's water-gate, a narrow lane running down from the town, and dropped a lesser line into the river to pick up whatever else offered. Here he was in good, leafy cover, and could stake himself into the bank and lie back to drowse until his line jerked him awake. From above, whether castle ramparts, town wall or upper window, he could not be seen.

It was beginning to grow dusk when he was startled wide awake by the hollow splash of something heavy plunging into the water, just upstream. Alert in a moment, he shoved off a yard or so from shore to look that way, but saw nothing to account for the sound, until an eddy in midstream showed him a dun-coloured sleeve breaking surface, and then the oval pallor of a face rising and sinking again from sight. A man's body turned slowly in the current as it sailed past. Madog was out after it instantly, his paddle plying. Getting a body from river into a coracle is a tricky business, but he had practised it so long that he had it perfect, balance and heft and all, from his first grasp on the billowing sleeve to the moment when the little boat bobbed like a cork and spun like a drifting leaf, with the drowned man in-board and streaming water. They were halfway across the river by that time, and there were half a dozen lay brothers just leaving their work in the vegetable gardens along the Gaye, on the other side, the nearest help in view. Madog made for their shore, and sent a halloo ahead of him to halt their departure and bring them running.

He had the salvaged man out on the bank by the time they reached him, and had turned him face-down into the grass and hoisted him firmly by the middle to shake the water out of him, squeezing energetically with big, gnarled hands.

'He's been in the river no more than a breath or two, I heard him souse into the water. Did you see ought over there by the water-gate?' But they shook their heads, concerned and anxious, and stooped to the drenched body, which at that instant heaved in breath, choked, and vomited the water it had swallowed. 'He's breathing. He'll do. But he was meant to drown, sure enough. See here!'

On the back of the head of thick, greying hair blood slowly seeped, along a broken and indented wound.

One of the lay brothers exclaimed aloud, and kneeled to turn up to the light the streaked and pallid face. 'Master William! This is our steward! He was collecting rents in the town . . . See, the pouch is gone from his belt!' Two rubbed and indented spots showed where the heavy satchel had bruised the leather beneath, and the lower edge of the stout belt itself showed a nick from a sharp knife, where the thongs had been sliced through in haste. 'Robbery and murder!'

'The one, surely, but not the other — not yet,' said Madog practically. 'He's breathing, you've not lost him yet. But we'd best get him to the nearest and best-tended bed, and that'll be in your infirmary, I take it. Make use of those hoes and spades of yours, lads, and here's a coat of mine to spare, if some of you will give up yours . . .'

They made a litter to carry Master William back to the abbey, as quickly and steadily as they could. Their entry at the gatehouse brought out porters, guests and brothers in alarm and concern. Brother Edmund the infirmarer came running and led the way to a bed beside the fire in the sick quarters. Jacob of Bouldon, rushing to confirm his fears, set up a distressed cry, but recovered himself gallantly, and ran for Brother Cadfael. The sub-prior, once informed of the circumstances by Madog, who was too accustomed to drowned and near-drowned men to get excited, sensibly sent a messenger hot-foot into the town to tell provost and sheriff what had happened, and the hunt was up almost before the victim was stripped of his soaked clothes, rolled in blankets and put to bed.

The sheriff's sergeant came, and listened to Madog's tale, with only a momentary narrowing of eyes at the fleeting suspicion that the tough old Welsh waterman might be adept at putting men into the water, as well as pulling them out. But in that case he would have been more likely to make sure that his victim went under, unless he was certain he could not name or identify his attacker. Madog saw the moment of doubt, and grinned scornfully.

'I get my living better ways. But if you need to question, there must be some among those gardeners from the Gaye who saw me come down-river and drop my line in under the trees there, and can tell you I never set foot ashore until I brought this one over, and shouted them to come and help with him. Maybe you don't know me, but these brothers here do.'

157

The sergeant, surely one of the few new enough to service in Shrewsbury castle to be ignorant of Madog's special position along the river, accepted Brother Edmund's warm assurances, and shrugged off his doubts.

'But sorry I am,' allowed Madog, mollified, 'that I neither saw nor heard anything until he plumped into the water, for I was drowsing. All I can say is that he went in upstream of me, but not far – I'd say someone slid him in from the cover of the water-gate.'

'A narrow, dark place, that,' said the sergeant.

'And a warren of passages above. And the light fading, though not far gone . . . Well, maybe when he comes round he'll be able to tell you something – he may have seen the man that did it.'

The sergeant settled down resignedly to wait for Master William to stir, which so far he showed no sign of doing. Cadfael had cleaned and bandaged the wound, dressing it with a herbal salve, and the steward lay with eyes closed and sunken, mouth painfully open upon snoring breath. Madog reclaimed his coat, which had been drying before the fire, and shrugged into it placidly. 'Let's hope nobody's thought the time right to help himself to my fish while my back was turned.' He had wrapped his salmon in an armful of wet grass and covered it with his upturned boat. 'I'll bid you goodnight, brothers, and wish your sick man hale again – and his pouch recovered, too, though that I doubt.'

From the infirmary doorway he turned back to say: 'You have a patient lad here sitting shivering on the doorstep, waiting for word. Can he not come in and see his master, he says. I've told him the man's likely to live his old age out with no worse than a dunt on the head to show for it, and he'd best be off to his bed, for he'll get nothing here as yet. Would you want him in?'

Cadfael went out with him to shoo away any such

premature visits. Jacob of Bouldon, pale and anxious, was sitting with arms folded closely round his drawn-up knees, hunched against the chill of the night. He looked up hopefully as they came out to him, and opened his mouth eagerly to plead. Madog clouted him amiably on the shoulder as he passed, and made off towards the gatehouse, a squat, square figure, brown and crusty as the bole of an oak.

'You'd best be off, too, into the warm,' said Brother Cadfael, not unkindly. 'Master William will recover well enough, but he's likely to be without his wits some time yet, no call for you to catch your death here on the stone.'

'I couldn't rest,' said Jacob earnestly. 'I told him, I begged him, take me with you, you should have someone. But he said, folly, he had collected rents for the abbey many years, and never felt any need for a guard. And now, see . . . Could I not come in and sit by him? I'd make no sound, never trouble him . . . He has not spoken?'

'Nor will for some hours yet, and even then I doubt he can tell us much. I'm here with him in case of need, and Brother Edmund is on call. The fewer about him, the better.'

'I'll wait a little while yet,' said Jacob, fretting, and hugged his knees the tighter.

Well, if he would, he would, but cramp and cold would teach him better sense and more patience. Cadfael went back to his vigil, and closed the door. Still, it was no bad thing to encounter one lad whose devotion gave the lie to Master William's forebodings concerning the younger generation.

Before midnight there was another visitor enquiring. The porter opened the door softly and came in to whisper that Master William's son was here, asking after his father and wanting to come in and see him. Since the sergeant, departing when it seemed certain his vigil was fruitless until morning, had pledged himself to go and reassure Mistress Rede that her man was alive, well cared for, and certain to make a good recovery, Cadfael might well have gone out to bid the young man go home and take care of his mother rather than waste his time here, if the young man had not forestalled him by making a silent and deter- mined entry on his herald's heels. A tall, shock-headed, dark-eyed youth, hunched of shoulder just now, and grim of face, but admittedly very quiet in movement, and low- voiced. His look was by no means tender or solicitous. His eyes went at once to the figure in the bed, sweaty-browed now, and breathing somewhat more easily and naturally. He brooded, glaring, and wasting no time on question or explanation, said in a level whisper: 'I will stay.' And with aggressive composure stayed, settling himself on the bench beside his father's bed, his two long, muscular hands gripped tightly between his knees.

The porter met Cadfael's eye, hoisted his shoulders, and went quietly away. Cadfael sat down on the other side of the bed, and contemplated the pair, father and son. Both faces looked equally aloof and critical, even hostile, yet there they were, close and quiet together.

The young man asked but two questions, each after a long silence. The first, uttered almost grudgingly, was: 'Will it be well with him?' Cadfael, watching the easing flow of breath and the faint flush of colour, said simply: 'Yes. Only give him time.' The second was: 'He has not spoken yet?'

'Not yet,' said Cadfael.

Now which of those, he wondered, was the more vital question? There was one man, somewhere, who must at this moment be very anxious indeed about what William Rede might have to say, when he did speak.

The young man – his name was Edward, Cadfael recalled, after the Confessor – Eddi Rede sat all night long almost motionless, brooding over his father's bed. Most of that time, and certainly every time he had been aware of being watched in his turn, he had been scowling.

Well before Prime the sergeant was back again to his watch, and Jacob was again hovering unhappily about the doorway, peering in anxiously whenever it was opened, but not quite venturing to come in until he was invited. The sergeant eyed Eddi very hard and steadily, but said no word to disturb the injured man's increasingly restful sleep. It was past seven when at last Master William stirred, opened vague eyes, made a few small sounds which were not yet words, and tried feebly to put up a hand to his painful head, startled by the sudden twinge when he moved. The sergeant stooped close, but Cadfael laid a restraining hand on his arm.

'Give him time! A knock on the head like that will have addled his wits. We'll need to tell him things before he tells us any.' And to the wondering patient he said tranquilly: 'You know me – Cadfael. Edmund will be here to relieve me as soon as Prime is over. You're in his care, in the infirmary, and past the worst. Fret for nothing, lie still and let others do that. You've had a mighty dunt on the crown, and a dowsing in the river, but both are past, and thanks be, you're safe enough now.'

The wandering hand reached its goal this time. Master William groaned and stared indignant surprise, and his eyes cleared and sharpened, though his voice was weak as he complained, with quickening memory: 'He came behind me – someone – out of an open yard door . . . That's the last I know . . .' Sudden realisation shook him; he gave a stricken howl, and tried to rise from his pillow, but gave up at the pang it cost him. 'The rents – the abbey rents!'

'Your life's better worth than the abbey rents,' said

Cadfael heartily, 'and even they may be regained.'

'The man who felled you,' said the sergeant, leaning close, 'cut your satchel loose with a knife, and made off with it. But if you can help us we'll lay him by the heels yet. Where was this that he struck you down?'

'Not a hundred paces from my own house,' lamented William bitterly. 'I went there when I had finished, to check my rolls and make all fast, and . . .' He shut his mouth grimly on the overriding reason. Hazily he had been aware all this time of the silent and sullen young man sitting beside him, now he fixed his eyes on him until his vision cleared. The mutual glare was spirited, and came of long practice. 'What are you doing here?' he demanded.

'Waiting to have better news of you to take to my mother,' said Eddi shortly. He looked up defiantly into the sergeant's face. 'He came home to read me all my sins over, and warn me that the fine that's due from me in two days more is my burden now, not his, and if I can't make shift for it on my own I may go to gaol, and pay in another coin. Or it may be,' he added with grudging fairness, 'that he came rather to flay me and then pay my dues, as he's done more than once. But I was in no mind to listen, and he was in no mind to be flouted, so I flung out and went down to the butts. And won the good half of what I owe, for what that's worth.'

'So this was a bitter quarrel you had between you,' said the sergeant, narrowing suspicious eyes. 'And not long after it you, master, went out to bring your rents home, and were set upon, robbed, and left for dead. And now you, boy, have the half of what you need to stay out of prison.'

Cadfael, watching father and son, felt that it had not even occurred to Eddi, until then, that he might fall under suspicion of this all too opportune attack; and further, that

162

even now it had not dawned on Master William that such a thought could occur to any sane man. He was scowling at his son for no worse reason than old custom and an aching head.

'Why are you not looking after your mother at home?' he demanded querulously.

'So I will, now I've seen and heard you more like yourself. Mother's well enough cared for, Cousin Alice is with her. But she'll be the better for knowing that you're still the same cantankerous worrit, and likely to be a plague to us twenty years yet. I'll go,' said Eddi grimly, 'when I'm let. But he wants your witness before he can leave you to your rest. Better get it said.'

Master William submitted wearily, knitting his brows in the effort to remember. 'I came from the house, along the passage towards Saint Mary's, above the water-gate. The door of the tanner's yard was standing open, I know – I'd passed it . . . But I never heard a step behind me. As if the wall had fallen on me! I recall nothing after, except sudden cold, deadly cold . . . Who brought me back, then, that I'm snug here?'

They told him, and he shook his head helplessly over the great blank between.

'You think the fellow must have been hiding behind that yard-door, lying in wait?'

'So it seems.'

'And you caught never a glimpse? Never had time to turn your head? You can tell us nothing to trace him? Not even a guess at his build? His age?'

Nothing. Simply, there had been early dusk before him, his own steps the only sound, no man in sight between the high walls of gardens, yards and warehouses going down to the river, and then the shock of the blow, and abrupt darkness. He was growing tired again, but his mind was clear enough. There would be no more to get from him.

Brother Edmund came in, eyed his patient, and silently nodded the visitors out at the door, to leave him in peace. Eddi kissed his father's dangling hand, but brusquely, rather as though he would as lief have bitten it, and marched out to blink at the sunlight in the great court. With a face grimly defiant he waited for the sergeant's dismissal.

'I left him as I told you, I went to the butts, and played into a wager there, and shot well. You'll want names from me. I can give them. And I'm still short the half of my fine, for what that's worth. I knew nothing of this until I went home, and that was late, after your messenger had been there. Can I go home? I'm at your disposal.'

'You can,' granted the sergeant, so readily that it was clear the young man would not be unwatched on the way, or on arrival. 'And there stay, for I shall want more from you than merely names. I'm away to take their tales from the lay brothers who were working late at the Gaye yesterday, but I'll not be long after you in the town.'

The workers were already assembling in the court and moving off to their day's labour. The sergeant strode forth to find his men, and left Eddi glowering after him, and Cadfael mildly observing the wary play of thought in the dark young face. Not a bad-looking lad, if he would wear a sunnier visage; but perhaps at this moment he had little cause.

'He will truly be a hale man again?' he asked suddenly, turning his black gaze on Cadfael.

'As whole and hearty as ever he was.'

'And you'll take good care of him?'

'So we will,' agreed Cadfael innocently, 'even though he may be a cantankerous worrit and a plague.'

'I'm sure none of you here have any call to say so,' flashed the young man with abrupt ferocity. 'The abbey has had loyal and solid service from him all these years,

164

and owes him more thanks than abuse.' And he turned his back and stalked away out of the great court, leaving Cadfael looking after him with a thoughtful face and the mere trace of a smile.

He was careful to wipe off the smile before he went back to Master William, who was in no mood to take himself, his son and his troubles anything but seriously. He lay trying to blink and frown away his headache, and fulminating about his offspring in a glum undertone.

'You see what I have to complain of, who should be able to look for comfort and support at home. A wild, unbiddable good-for-nothing, and insolent into the bargain . . .'

'So he is,' agreed Cadfael sympathetically, wooden-faced. 'No wonder you mean to let him pay for his follies in prison, and small blame to you.'

He got an acid glare as reward. 'I shall do no such thing!' snapped Master William sharply. 'The boy's no worse than you or I at his age, I daresay. Nothing wrong with him that time won't cure.'

Master William's disaster, it seemed, had shaken the serenity of the abbey from choir to guest-hall. The enquirers were many and assiduous. Young Jacob had been hopping about outside the infirmary from dawn, unable to tear himself away even to the duties he owed his injured master, until Cadfael had taken pity on his obvious anxiety, and stopped to tell him that there was no need for such distress, for the worst was over, and all would be well with Master William.

'You are sure, brother? He has regained his senses? He has spoken? His mind is clear?'

Patiently Cadfael repeated his reassurances.

'But such villainy! Has he been able to help the sheriff's men? Did he see his attacker? Has he any notion who it could have been?'

'Not that, no. Never a glimpse, he was struck from behind, and knew no more until he came to this morning in the infirmary. He's no help to the law, I fear. It was not to be expected.'

'But he himself will be well and strong again?'

'As ever he was, and before long, too.'

'Thank God, brother!' said Jacob fervently, and went away satisfied to his accounts. For even with the town rents lost, there was still book-work to be done on what remained.

More surprising it seemed to be stopped on the way to the dortoir by Warin Harefoot, the haberdasher, with a very civil enquiry after the steward's health. Warin did not presume to display the agitation of a favoured colleague like Jacob, but rather the mannerly sympathy of a humble guest of the house, and the law-abiding citizen's indigna-tion at evil-doing, and desire that justice should pursue the evildoer. Had his honour been able to put a name or a face to his attacker? A great pity! Yet justice, he hoped, might still be done. And would there – should any man be so fortunate as to trace the missing satchel with its treasure – would there be a small reward for such a service? To an honest man who restored it, Cadfael thought, there well might. Warin went off to his day's peddling in Shrewsbury, humping his heavy pack. The back view of him, for some reason, looked both pur-poseful and jaunty.

But the strangest and most disturbing enquirer made, in fact, no enquiry, but came silently in, as Cadfael was paying another brief visit to the infirmary in the early afternoon, after catching up with some of his lost sleep. Brother Eutropius stood motionless and intent at the foot of the steward's bed, staring down with great hollow eyes in a face like a stone mask. He gave never a glance to

Cadfael. All he regarded was the sleeping man, now so placid and eased for all his bandaged head, a man back from the river, back from the grave. He stood there for a long time, his lips moving on inaudible formulae of prayer. Suddenly he shuddered, like someone waking from a trance, and crossed himself, and went away as silently as he had come.

Cadfael was so concerned at his manner and his closed face that he went out after him, no less quietly, and followed him at distance through the cloisters and into the church.

Brother Eutropius was on his knees before the high altar, his marble face upraised over clasped hands. His eyelids were closed, but the dark lashes glittered. A handsome, agonised man of thirty, with a strong body and a fierce, tormented heart, his lips framing silently but readably in the altar-light: '*Mea culpa . . . maxima mea culpa . . .*'

Cadfael would have liked to pierce the distance and the ice between, but it was not the time. He went away quietly, and left Brother Eutropius to the remnant of his disrupted solitude, for whatever had happened to him, the shell was cracked and disintegrating, and never again would he be able to reassemble it about him.

Cadfael went into the town before Vespers, to call upon Mistress Rede, and take her the latest good word of her man. It was by chance that he met the sergeant at the High Cross, and stopped to exchange news. It had been a routine precaution to round up a few of the best-known rogues in Shrewsbury, and make them account for their movements the previous day, but that had yielded nothing. Eddi's fellow-marksmen at the butts under the town wall had sworn to his story willingly, but seeing they were all his cronies from boyhood, that meant little enough. The one new thing, and it marked the exact spot of the attack past question, was the discovery in the passage above the water-gate of the one loop of leather from Master William's pouch, the one which had been sliced clean through and left lying in the thief's haste, and the dim light under the high walls.

'Right under the clothier's cart-yard. The walls are ten feet high, and the passage narrow. Never a place from which the lane can be overlooked. No chance in the world of an eye witness. He chose his place well.'

'Ah, but there *is* one place, then, from which a man might have watched the deed,' said Cadfael, enlightened. 'The loft above that cart-house and barn has a hatch higher than the wall, and close to it. And Roger Clothier lets Rhodri Fychan sleep up there – the old Welshman who begs at Saint Mary's church. By that time of the evening he may have been up in the hay already, and on a fine evening he'd be sitting by the open hatch. And even if he had not come home at that time, who's to be sure of that? It's enough that he *could* have been there . . .'

He had been right about the sergeant; the man was an incomer, not yet acquainted with the half of what went on in Shrewsbury. He had not known Madog of the Dead-Boat, he did not know Rhodri Fychan. Pure chance had cast this particular affair into the hands of such a man, and perhaps no ill chance, either.

'You have given me a notion,' said Cadfael, 'that may bring us nearer the truth yet. Not that I'd let the old man run any risk, but no need for that. Listen, there's a baited trap we might try, if you're agreeable. If it succeeds you may have your man. If it fails, we shall have lost nothing. But it's a matter of doing it quietly – no public proclamation, leave the baiting to me. Will you give it a trial? It's your credit if we hook our fish, and it costs but a night-watch.'

The sergeant stared, already sniffing at the hope of praise and promotion, but cautious still. 'What is it you have in mind?'

'Say you had done this thing, there between blind walls, and then suddenly heard that an old man slept above every night of the year, and may have been there when you struck. And say you were told that this old beggar has not yet been questioned —but tomorrow he will be . . .'

'Brother,' said the sergeant, 'I am with you. I am listening.'

There were two things to be done, after that, if the spring was to succeed, and imperil no one but the guilty. No need to worry, as yet, about getting permission to be absent in the night, or, failing that, making his own practised but deprecated way out without permission. Though he had confidence in Abbot Radulfus, who had, before now, shown confidence in him. Justice is a permitted passion, the just respect it. Meantime, Cadfael went up to Saint Mary's churchyard, and sought out the venerable beggar who sat beside the west door, in his privileged and honoured place.

Rhodri the Less — for his father had been Rhodri, too, and a respected beggar like his son — knew the footstep, and turned up a wrinkled and pock-marked face, brown as the soil, smiling.

'Brother Cadfael, well met, and what's the news with you?'

Cadfael sat down beside him, and took his time. 'You'll have heard of this bad business that was done right under your bedchamber, yesterday evening. Were you there, last night?'

'Not when this befell,' said the old man, scratching his white poll thoughtfully, 'and can find no one who was down there at that time, either. Last night I begged late, it was a mild evening. Vespers was over and gone here before I went home.'

'No matter,' said Cadfael. 'Now listen, friend, for I'm borrowing your nest tonight, and you'll be a guest else-where, if you'll be my helper . . .'

'For a Welshman,' said the old man comfortably, 'what-ever he asks. You need only tell me.' But when it was told, he shook his head firmly. 'There's an inner loft. In the worst of the winter I move in there for the warmth, away from the frosty air. Why should not I be present? There's a door between, and room for you and more. And I should like, Brother Cadfael, I should like of all things to be witness when Will Rede's murderer gets his come-uppance.'

He leaned to rattle his begging-bowl at a pious lady who had been putting up prayers in the church. Business was business, and the pitch he held was the envy of the beggars of Shrewsbury. He blessed the giver, and reached a delaying hand to halt Cadfael, who was rising to depart.

'Brother, a word for you that might come helpfully, who knows! They are saying that one of your monks was down under the bridge yesterday evening, about the time Madog took up Will out of the water. They say he stood there under the stone a long time, like a man in a dream, but no good dream. One they know but very little, a man in his prime, dark-avised, solitary . . .'

'He came late to Vespers,' said Cadfael, remembering.

'You know I have those who tell me things, for no evil purpose – a man who sits still must have the world come to him. They tell me this brother walked into the water, above his sandals, and would have gone deeper, but it was then Madog of the Dead-Boat hallooed that he had a drowned man aboard. And the strange monk drew back out of the water and fled from his devil. So they say. Does it mean anything to you?'

170

'Yes,' said Cadfael slowly. 'Yes, it means much.'

When Cadfael had finished reassuring the steward's brisk, birdlike little wife that she should have her man back in a day or two as good as new, he drew Eddi out with him into the yard, and told him all that was in the wind.

'And I am off back now to drop the quiet word into a few ears I can think of, where it may raise the fiercest itch. But not too early, or why should not the thought be passed on to the sheriff's man at once for action? No, last thing, after dark, when all good brothers are making their peace with the day before bed, I shall have recalled that there's one place from which yonder lane can be overlooked, and one man who sleeps the nights there, year-round, and may have things to tell. First thing tomorrow, I shall let them know, I'll send the sheriff the word, and let him deal. Whoever fears an eye-witness shall have but this one night to act.'

The young man eyed him with a doubtful face but a glint in his glance. 'Since you can hardly expect to take *me* in that trap, brother, I reckon you have another use for me.'

'This is your father. If you will, you may be with the witnesses in the rear loft. But mark, I do not know, no one can know yet, that the bait will fetch any man.'

'And if it does not,' said Eddi with a wry grin, 'if no one comes, I can still find the hunt hard on my heels.'

'True! But if it succeeds . . .'

He nodded grimly. 'Either way, I have nothing to lose. But listen, one thing I want amended, or I'll spring your trap before the time. It is not I who will be in the rear loft with Rhodri Fychan and your sergeant. It is *you*. I shall be the sleeper in the straw, waiting for a murderer. You said rightly, brother – this is *my* father. Mine, not yours!'

This had been no part of Brother Cadfael's plans, but

for all that, he found it did not greatly surprise him. Nor, by the set of the intent young face and the tone of the quiet voice, did he think demur would do much good. But he tried.

'Son, since it *is* your father, think better of it. He'll have need of you. A man who has tried once to kill will want to make certain this time. He'll come with a knife, if he comes at all. And you, however sharp your ears and stout your heart, still at a disadvantage, lying in a feigned sleep . . .'

'And are your senses any quicker than mine, and your sinews any suppler and stronger?' Eddi grinned suddenly, and clapped him on the shoulder with a large and able hand. 'Never fret, brother, I am well prepared for when that man and I come to grips. You go and sow your good seed, and may it bear fruit! I'll make ready.'

When robbery and attempted murder are but a day and a half old, and still the sensation of a whole community, it is by no means difficult to introduce the subject and insert into the speculations whatever new crumb of interest you may wish to propagate. As Cadfael found, going about his private business in the half-hour after Compline. He did not have to introduce the subject, in fact, for no one was talking about anything else. The only slight difficulty was in confiding his sudden idea to each man in solitude, since any general announcement would at once have caused some native to blurt out the obvious objection, and give the entire game away. But even that gave little trouble, for certainly the right man, if he really was among those approached, would not say one word of it to anyone else, and would have far too much to think about to want company or conversation the rest of the night.

Young Jacob, emerging cramped and yawning after hours of assiduous scribing, broken only by snatched meals and a dutiful visit to his master, now sitting up by the infirmary hearth, received Brother Cadfael's sudden idea wide-eyed and eager, and offered, indeed, to hurry to the castle even at this late hour to tell the watch about it, but Cadfael considered that hard-working officers of the law might be none too grateful at having their night's rest disrupted; and in any case nothing would be changed by morning.

To half a dozen guests of the commoners' hall, who came to make kind enquiry after Master William, he let fall his idea openly, as a simple possibility, since none of them was a Shrewsbury man, or likely to know too much about the inhabitants. Warin Harefoot was among the six, and perhaps the instigator of the civil gesture. He looked, as always, humble, zealous, and pleased at any motion, even the slightest, towards justice.

There remained one mysterious and troubled figure. Surely not a murderer, not even quite a self-murderer, though by all the signs he had come very close. But for Madog's cry of: 'Drowned man!' he might indeed have waded into the full flow of the stream and let it take him. It was as if God himself had set before him, like a lightning stroke from heaven, the enormity of the act he contemplated, and driven him back from the brink with the dazzle of hell-fire. But those who returned stricken and penitent to face this world had need also of men, and the communicated warmth of men.

Before Cadfael so much as opened the infirmary door, on a last visit to the patient within, he had a premonition of what he would find. Master William and Brother Eutropius sat companionably one on either side of the hearth, talking together in low, considerate voices, with silences as acceptable as speech, and speech no more eloquent than the silences. There was no defining the thread that linked them, but there would never be any breaking it. Cadfael would have withdrawn unnoticed, but the slight creak of the door drew Brother Eutropius' attention, and he rose to take his leave.

'Yes, brother, I know – I've overstayed. I'll come.'

It was time to withdraw to the dortoir and their cells, and sleep the sleep of men at peace. And Eutropius, as he fell in beside Cadfael in the great court, had the face of a man utterly at peace. Drained, still dazed by the thunderbolt of revelation, but already, surely, confessed and absolved. Empty now, and still a little at a loss in reaching out a hand to a fellow-man.

'Brother, I think it was you who came into the church, this afternoon. I am sorry if I caused you anxiety. I had but newly looked my fault in the face. It seemed to me that my sin had all but killed another, an innocent, man. Brother, I have long known in my head that despair is mortal sin. Now I know it with my blood and bowels and heart.'

Cadfael said, stepping delicately: 'No sin is mortal, if it is deeply and truly repented. He lives, and you live. You need not see your case as extreme, brother. Many a man has fled from grief into the cloister, only to find that grief can follow him there.'

'There was a woman . . .' said Eutropius, his voice low, laboured but calm. 'Until now I could not speak of this. A woman who played me false, bitterly, yet I could not leave loving. Without her my life seemed of no worth. I know its value better now. For the years left to me I will pay its price in full, and carry it without complaint.'

To him Cadfael said nothing more. If there was one man in all this web of guilt and innocence who would sleep deeply and well in his own bed that night, it was Brother Eutropius.

As for Cadfael himself, he had best make haste to take

advantage of his leave of absence, and get to the clothier's loft by the shortest way, for it was fully dark, and if the bait had been taken the end could not long be delayed.

The steep ladder had been left where it always leaned, against the wall below Rhodri's hatch. In the outer loft the darkness was not quite complete, for the square of the hatch stood open as always on a space of starlit sky. The air within was fresh, but warm and fragrant with the dry, heaped hay and straw, stored from the previous summer, and dwindling now from the winter's depredations, but still ample for a comfortable bed. Eddi lay stretched out on his left side, turned towards the square of luminous sky, his right arm flung up round his head, to give him cover as he kept watch.

In the inner loft, with the door ajar between to let sounds pass, Brother Cadfael, the sergeant, and Rhodri Fychan sat waiting, with lantern, flint and steel ready to hand. They had more than an hour to wait. If he was coming at all, he had had the cold patience and self-control to wait for the thick of the night, when sleep is deepest.

But come he did, when Cadfael, for one, had begun to think their fish had refused the bait. It must have been two o'clock in the morning, or past, when Eddi, watching steadily beneath his sheltering arm, saw the level base of the square of sky broken, as the crown of a head rose into view, black against darkest blue, but clear to eyes already inured to darkness. He lay braced and still, and tuned his breathing to the long, impervious rhythm of sleep, as the head rose stealthily, and the intruder paused for a long time, head and shoulders in view, motionless, listening. The silhouette of a man has neither age nor colouring, only a shape. He might have been twenty or fifty, there was no knowing. He could move with formidable silence.

175

But he was satisfied. He had caught the steady sound of breathing, and now with surprising speed mounted the last rungs of the ladder and was in through the hatch, and the bulk of him cut off the light. Then he was still again, to make sure the movement had not disturbed the sleeper. Eddi was listening no less acutely, and heard the infinitely small whisper of steel sliding from its sheath. A dagger is the most silent of weapons to use, but has its own voices. Eddi turned very slightly, with wincing care, to free his left arm under him, ready for the grapple.

The bulk and shadow, a moving darkness, mere sensation rather than anything seen, drew close. He felt the leaning warmth from a man's body, and the stirring of the air from his garments, and was aware of a left hand and arm outstretched with care to find how he lay, hovering rather than touching. He had time to sense how the assassin stooped, and judge where his right hand lay waiting with the knife, while the left selected the place to strike. Under the sacking that covered him – for beggars do not lie in good woollens – Eddi braced himself to meet the shock.

When the blow came, there was even a splinter of light tracing the lunge of the blade, as the murderer drew back to put his weight into the stroke, and uncovered half the blessed frame of sky. Eddi flung over on his back, and took the lunging dagger-hand cleanly by the wrist in his left hand. He surged out of the straw ferociously, forcing the knife away at arm's length, and with his right hand reached for and found his opponent's throat. They rolled out of the nest of rustling straw and across the floor, struggling, and fetched up against the timbers of the wall. The attacker had uttered one startled, muted cry before he was half-choked. Eddi had made no sound at all but the fury of his movements. He let himself be clawed by his enemy's flailing left hand, while he laid both hands to get

176

possession of the dagger. With all his strength he dashed the elbow of the arm he held against the floor. A strangled yelp answered him, the nerveless fingers parted, and gave up the knife. Eddi sat back astride a body suddenly limp and gasping, and laid the blade above a face still nameless.

In the inner loft the sergeant had started up and laid hand to the door, but Cadfael took him by the arm and held him still.

The feverish whisper reached them clearly, but whispers have neither sex nor age nor character. 'Don't strike – wait, listen!' He was terrified, but still thinking, still scheming. 'It *is* you – I know you, I've heard about you . . . his son! Don't kill me – why should you? It wasn't you I expected – I never meant *you* harm . . .'

What you may have heard about him, thought Cadfael, braced behind the door with his hand on the tinder-box he might need at any moment, may be as misleading as common report so often is. There are overtones and undertones to be listened for, that not every ear can catch.

'Lie still,' said Eddi's voice, perilously calm and reasonable, 'and say what you have to say where you lie. I can listen just as well with this toy at your throat. Have I said I mean to kill you?'

'But do not!' begged the eager voice, breathless and low. Cadfael knew it, now. The sergeant probably did not. In all likelihood Rhodri Fychan, leaning close and recording all, had never heard it, or he would have known it, for his ears could pick up even the shrillest note of the bat. 'I can do you good. You have a fine unpaid, and only a day to run before gaol. *He* told me so. What do you owe him? He would not clear you, would he? But I can see you cleared. Listen, never say word of this, loose me and keep your own counsel, and the half is yours – the half of the abbey rents. I promise it!'

There was a blank silence. If Eddi was tempted, it was certainly not to bargain, more likely to strike, but he held his hand, at whatever cost.

'Join me,' urged the voice, taking heart from his silence, 'and no one need ever know. No one! They said there was a beggar slept here, but he's away, however it comes, and no one here but you and I, to know what befell. Even if they were using you, think better of it, and who's to know? Only let me go hence, and you keep a close mouth, and all's yet well, for you as well as me.'

After another bleak silence Eddi's voice said with cold suspicion. 'Let you loose, and you the only one who knows where you've hidden the plunder? Do you take me for a fool? I should never see my share! Tell me the place, exact, and bring me to it with you, or I give you to the law.'

The listeners within felt, rather than heard, the faint sounds of writhing and struggling and baulking, like a horse resisting a rider, and then the sudden collapse, the abject surrender. 'I put the money into my pouch with my own few marks,' owned the voice bitterly, 'and threw his satchel into the river. The money is in my bed in the abbey. No one paid any heed to my entry with the Foregate dues remaining, why should they? And those I've accounted for properly. Come down with me, and I'll satisfy you, I'll pay you. More than the half, if you'll only keep your mouth shut, and let me go free . . .'

'You within there,' suddenly bellowed Eddi, shaking with detestation, 'come forth, for the love of God, and take this carrion away from under me, before I cut his villain throat, and rob the hangman of his own. Come out, and see what we've caught!'

And out they came, the sergeant to thrust across at once to bar any escape by the hatch, Cadfael to set his lantern safely on a beam well clear of the hay and straw, and tap away diligently with flint and steel until the tinder caught and glowed, and the wick burned up into a tiny flame. Eddi's captive had uttered one despairing oath, and made one frantic effort to throw off the weight that held him down and break for the open air, but was flattened back to the boards with a thump, a large, vengeful hand splayed on his chest.

'He dares, he dares,' Eddi was grating through his teeth, 'to try and buy my father's head from me with money – stolen money, abbey money! You heard? You heard?'

The sergeant leaned from the hatch and whistled for the two men he had had in hiding below in the barn. He was glad he had given the plan a hearing. The injured man live and mending well, the money located and safe – everything would redound to his credit. Now send the prisoner bound and helpless with his escort to the castle, and off to the abbey to unearth the money.

The guarded flame of the lantern burned up and cast a yellow light about the loft. Eddi rose and stood back from his enemy, who sat up slowly and sullenly, still breathless and bruised, and blinked round them all with the large, ingenuous eyes and round, youthful face of Jacob of Bouldon, that paragon of clerks, so quick to learn the value of a rent-roll, so earnest to win the trust and approval of his master, and lift from him every burden, particularly the burden of a full satchel of the abbey's dues.

He was grazed and dusty now, and the cheerful, lively mask had shrivelled into hostile and malevolent despair. With flickering, sidelong glances he viewed them all, and saw no way out of the circle. Longest he looked at the little, spry, bowed old man who came forth smiling at Cadfael's shoulder. For in the wrinkled, lively face the lantern-light showed two eyes that caught reflected light though they had none of their own, eyes opaque as grey pebbles and as insensitive. Jacob stared and moaned,

and softly and viciously began to curse.

'Yes,' said Brother Cadfael, 'you might have saved yourself so vain an effort. I fear I was forced to practise a measure of deceit, which would hardly have taken in a true-born Shrewsbury man. Rhodri Fychan has been blind from birth.'

It was in some way an apt ending, when Brother Cadfael and the sergeant arrived back at the abbey gatehouse, about first light, to find Warin Harefoot waiting in the porter's room for the bell for Prime to rouse the household and deliver him of his charge, which he had brought here for safety in the night. He was seated on a bench by the empty hearth, one hand clutching firmly at the neck of a coarse canvas sack.

'He has not let go of it all night,' said the porter, 'nor let me leave sitting t'other side of it as guard.'

Warin was willing enough, however, even relieved, to hand over his responsibility to the law, with a monk of the house for witness, seeing abbot and prior were not yet up to take precedence. He undid the neck of the sack proudly, and displayed the coins within.

'You did say, brother, there might be a reward, if a man was so lucky as to find it. I had my doubts of that young clerk – I never trust a too-honest face! And if it *was* he – well, I reasoned he must hide what he stole quickly. And he had a pouch on him the like of the other, near enough, and nobody was going to wonder at seeing him wearing it, or having money in it, either, seeing he had a small round of his own. And if he came a thought late, well, he'd made a point he might make a slower job of it than he'd expected, being a novice at the collecting. So I kept my eye on him, and got my chance this night, when I saw him creep forth after dark. In his bed it was, sewn into a corner of the straw pallet. And here it is, and speak for me

180

with the lord abbot. Trade's none so good, and a poor pedlar must live . . .'

Gaping down at him long and wonderingly, the sergeant questioned at last: 'And did you never for a moment consider slipping the whole into your own pack, and out through the gates with it in the morning?'

Warin cast up a shy, disarming glance. 'Well, sir, for a moment it may be I did. But I was never the lucky sort if I did the like, never a once but I was found out. Wisdom and experience turned me honest. Better, I hold, a small profit come by honestly than great gains gone down the wind, and me in prison for it just the same. So here's the abbey's gold again, every penny, and now I look to the lord abbot to treat a poor, decent man fair.'

Miles Tripp

RAGSIE'S MISTRESS

Young and healthy, spending their first night in their newly purchased house in an upmarket residential district, they were supremely happy. Seated on scatter cushions sipping black coffee and Drambuie they leafed through a contact magazine which his partner in an advertising agency had given him. They read it for laughs; they were far too satisfied with each other and themselves to need the novelty of swapping or troilism.

'The code words baffle me,' she said. 'What is B and D? And what on earth does "proficient in O levels" mean?'

'I'm reading it with a cold professional eye,' he replied. ' "He vasectomised, 6 footer; she petite, 37-25-35". Sounds like a Tarzan and Jane duo.'

She put the magazine aside and appraised him lovingly. 'He Clive, very handsome, top executive.'

He gave her a light kiss and responded with 'She Jill, beautiful, sexy, clever research scientist.'

The silence of complete contentment was broken when, staring at flickering shadows thrown by an electric fire, she said, 'Let's unblock the fireplace and have real fires.'

He weighed her suggestion. 'It would make work. Ashes. Dust.'

'But it would look so nice. And it would be lovely in winter. Just think. We could curl up on a rug in front of a glowing log fire. It's not the same in front of an electric one.'

'If we had a real fire now I'd sling that on it,' he said nodding towards the magazine. 'I'm not sharing my wife with anyone.'

'You agree then? We'll convert it into a fireplace?'

'We'll have it restored. But on one condition. It's not going to be a D.I.Y. job. I'll get a builder along.'

'But you're the man who enjoys building walls. Who used to quote Winston Churchill on brick-laying as a marvellous recreation?'

'That was building, not demolishing.'

She teased him gently for a minute or two about the wall he had built at their previous home and when the teasing became too provocative he made a grab at her.

'Not in here,' she smiled. 'Not now. Wait till we've got a fire burning in the hearth.'

Within a month they had a deep open fireplace but they also had an unsolved mystery. When the builder had removed plaster and brickwork to expose the original grate he had found a wooden crate. On breaking open the crate he found the skeleton of a large dog inside. 'Can't understand it,' he said to Clive. 'Who'd want to bury a pooch under a chimney?'

'Santa Claus maybe. Emergency meat ration for reindeer.'

The builder laughed but Jill didn't. 'It was probably a much-loved pet the owner couldn't bear to bury,' she said.

'It'll get buried now. At the top of our garden.'

'I'll give you a hand,' said the builder.

Later, when she was preparing their evening meal, Jill remarked, 'A skeleton in the hearth makes a change from a skeleton in the cupboard.'

'Every family has at least one. And a black sheep as well.'

'Mine hasn't,' she said, reaching for a jar of tarragon. 'But you know what a dull lot of relations I've got. How about yours?'

'The same. Ditchwater sparkles by comparison. But no longer. Now we're like everyone else. We've got a genuine skeleton.'

She shook her head. 'Not like everyone else. Nobody could possibly be as happy as we are.'

A white goatskin rug lay in front of the fire. He dimmed the lights and shadows flickered on the walls. Gently he drew her towards him, but she pulled away. 'In bed,' she whispered.

'But I thought . . .'

'So did I. But it's different now.'

'I don't get it.' The puzzled tone of his voice didn't altogether disguise his disappointment.

'I know it's silly, and it doesn't bother me – honestly it doesn't – but it's that silly skeleton. I don't think it would be watching me or anything neurotic like that but I don't want to start thinking about it . . . Well, in the middle . . .'

'I understand.'

'You do?'

'Completely.'

'Normally I don't think about it at all. But I don't want suddenly to start thinking of it when we're . . .'

He placed his hand over her mouth. 'No explanations necessary. Anyway, bed is the proper place.'

She removed his hand. 'Anywhere with you is the proper place, but not here, not tonight.'

It was just before three in the morning that they were both woken by a strange noise from outside. It sounded like a dog's dolorous howl. He opened the window and peered out. There was nothing to be seen even though the garden was flooded by moonlight. The howling stopped and he went back to bed.

Before leaving for work they asked a neighbour if there was a dog in the avenue which made a noise at night but were told that the only dogs were small household pets.

The neighbour hadn't heard anything.

Four nights passed without incident but on the fifth they were again woken by woeful baying. Again Clive opened the window and the noise stopped. At breakfast they made a joke of it. 'Whoever heard of a garden being haunted by a dog?' but there was an edge of nervousness to Jill's laughter.

A week went by and then, in the early hours of a Monday morning, Clive felt his wife shaking him awake.

'What's the matter,' he asked sleepily.

'There's something downstairs. A sort of scratching at the back door.'

He switched on the bedside light. 'Scratching?'

'Listen.'

From below came a faint but insistent scraping sound as though some animal was running its claws down the outside of the door.

'It wants to be let in,' she whispered.

'Wants to be let in! You must be joking!' His voice was rough with displeased incredulity.

'Are you going down?'

He threw back the bedclothes with the violence of a man who has just been told he has been sleeping in contaminated sheets.

'I'll go all right.'

'It's stopped now.'

'I'm still going.' He slipped on a dressing gown. 'If I'm not back in ten minutes send out a search party.'

A look of annoyance flashed across her face. 'It isn't funny.'

'I'll say it's not. I need to be sharp and fresh in the morning, not a sleep-starved zombie.'

The moment the door closed after him she reached out and opened a drawer in the bedside table. She took out a small bottle and shook out a couple of pills on to the palm of her hand. These were tranquillisers which her doctor

186

had prescribed when she had gone to him complaining of sudden attacks of anxiety and panic which came for no apparent reason. She wondered if work pressures were responsible for these feelings. As a research scientist with a cosmetics company she was being pushed to meet a deadline which had been fixed for the marketing of a new range of perfumes. And the pressure had been exacerbated by the attentions of an animal welfare organisation which was trying to make the public boycott the company's products while these were being tested on animals. Before these protests were made she had regarded rabbits and mice with scientific detachment but now it was becoming more difficult to remain emotionally detached and to see the animals with scientific objectivity as insensate expendable units of research.

She didn't believe the strange howling at night was connected with her work, and she wasn't superstitious or afraid of supernatural phenomena, but she felt acutely uneasy and was unable to pin down the reason for her disquiet. She and Clive were happy together, both had jobs they liked and were well paid for doing, and yet she had the feeling that their contentment was being stalked by a malign force which would strike when least expected.

He came back within the ten minute span. 'Not a thing to be seen. And no marks on the door.'

He climbed back into bed and turned his back on her.

The tranquillisers did their duty. She was soon asleep. She slept so soundly that he had to wake her when it was time to get up.

They snatched a breakfast as both were late.

She went to the sitting room to collect some papers while he put on his coat, ready to go to the garage.

'Clive,' she called.

He was almost out of the house. 'Yes?'

'Come here a sec.'

He didn't attempt to mask his irritation when he

entered the room. 'We're late. What the hell is it?'

'Look,' She pointed.

'I'm looking.'

'Don't you notice anything?'

'We are late.' Each syllable sounded as though it were heavily underlined.

'Look at the rug.'

'What about the rug? It's a rug. Our rug. It's the same rug. It hasn't flown away. It's a static self-respecting rug not some bloody aerodynamic carpet.'

'It's crumpled at the end.'

'So what? Straighten it out if it bothers you.'

'It was straight when we went to bed last night. It's been crumpled since we went to bed.'

'Nonsense.'

She used self-control to keep her voice even-tempered. 'It isn't nonsense. And the cushion from the chair was on the floor beside it.'

'What cushion?'

'That one. I've put it back now. But it was on the floor by the rug.'

He shook his head.

'I could swear someone or something has been sleeping there,' she went on.

'Maybe. Maybe. We'll talk about it tonight, shall we? I'm late. You're late. Let's go now. Okay?'

He walked towards the door.

'Do you think,' she began. But he had gone.

They didn't talk about it that night because they went to a party at a friend's house and the subject was never raised. The party didn't break up until two in the morning and they were undressing when they heard a furious barking from downstairs. Clive, wearing only underpants and socks, ran down and was just in time to see a man retreating through an open front window. He glanced around. No objects had been disturbed or stolen. The intruder had obviously been scared away by the barking dog. But there was no sign of a dog.

Jill joined him in the sitting room. He told her what he had seen.

'I wonder if the man, whoever he was, was responsible for mussing up the rug last night,' she said. 'Maybe he was using this place as a pad.'

'I'm going to call the police.'

'Why? Nothing's been taken.'

He gave her an incredulous look. 'Our house has been broken into. Of course it must be reported.'

'And you'll tell them about the dog? And how it scared the burglar away?'

He gave a laugh which was as false as a cracked bell. 'Dog? There isn't a dog. If I start talking about a dog they'll think we're mad. I shan't say anything about a dog.'

'For all you know it saved our lives.'

He placed his hands on her shoulders. 'Listen, darling. There is no dog. I shall simply say I heard a noise, came to investigate and disturbed a burglar.'

'And we shall get questions; hassle. Please don't. We haven't lost anything.'

'I think we should. Apart from anything else, it's public spirited.'

It was her turn to laugh and her laugh was as false as his had been. 'Public spirited. Since when has the man who fakes his tax returns, lies about products he knows shouldn't be on sale let alone advertised, breaks every traffic regulation, been public spirited?'

He took his hands from her shoulders as though they had been resting on an oven hot-plate.

'Thanks very much. It's nice to have the admiration and support of one's wife.'

She turned away. 'I'm going to bed. You do what you want. But if you do call the police I shall tell them about the dog and to hell whether they think we're round the bend.'

He didn't inform the police. At breakfast next morning they hardly spoke to each other. Unhappily each went to work; he to an office in the city, she to a laboratory in the outskirts.

During her lunch-hour she visited a nearby super-market and bought a packet of dog biscuits. Arriving home before her husband she put some biscuits in a dish in the kitchen.

At first he didn't notice the dish and it was only when he dropped a cup and was picking up shattered pieces that he saw it.

'What the devil is that?'

'What does it look like,' she replied defiantly.

'Are you sure you're feeling all right?'

Her eyes blazed. 'Who's being supportive and admiring?'

He spoke slowly and deliberately. 'We have heard some strange noises. Dog-like noises. There is no doubt an explanation for these. We certainly haven't seen a dog. Moreover, you have been working very hard lately and your company is heavily under pressure from a vociferous anti-vivisection organisation. It's understandable that the noises plus the skeleton plus your working conditions have been playing on your mind. It's understandable . . .'

'If you use that word again,' she screamed, 'I swear I'll leave you. I don't want understanding. I understand me and I'm not going mad.'

'Who said you were? I didn't. I said it was under-standable.'

She was almost crying with anger. 'That does it,' she sobbed. 'You can sleep in the spare room tonight. I don't want you near me. Good night.'

She ran from the kitchen, ran upstairs, and he heard a key turn in the bedroom door.

He looked at the bits of broken cup in his hand, and then at the dish of dog biscuits. 'Christ,' he said.

Next morning while they were having breakfast she reached across the table for his hand. For a moment they held hands. 'I'm sorry,' she said. 'The biscuits haven't been eaten.'

He gave her hand a squeeze. 'No. I don't think there's anything to eat them.'

She gave a tired smile. She had slept very badly. 'You're right. Perhaps I've been going at it too hard. I'll put the biscuits away. I don't know why I bought them in the first place. I was just . . .'

'You thought there was a dog and you wanted to be friendly.'

'That's it.' Her smile lightened. 'You are an understanding man, and I love you.'

'Our first big quarrel and hopefully our last.'

'Our very last,' she affirmed.

That night they went to bed together and made love. Lying in his arms she said, 'I've been a fool. I really meant it when I said I'd walk out on you.' She turned to kiss his cheek. '*That* would have been mad.'

He caressed her hair. 'I love you for you, whatever happens.' He was about to say something else when they were distracted by a scratching noise.

It was on the outside of the bedroom door.

They held each other tight.

The scratching continued.

She pulled away. 'I'm going to settle this once and for all.'

She ran across the room and opened the door.

There was nothing outside.

He joined her and switched on the landing light. There were no marks on the carpet or door, and nothing to show that there had been a presence. Together they went to the bathroom. It was undisturbed but a tap was dripping slowly. He turned it off. 'It couldn't have been that,' he said. 'It wasn't a dripping noise.'

'This place is haunted,' she replied with a nervous laugh. 'Let's get back to bed.'

He led the way but stopped as soon as he entered the bedroom. She followed his gaze. There was an imprint at the foot of the bed as though something had been lying on the covering.

'Oh, well,' she said, 'that shows he's friendly. He's sharing our bed.'

'What did you say?'

'You heard.'

'He's sharing our bed? Who's supposed to be sharing our bed?'

'You know what I mean.'

'You said *he*. "He's sharing our bed." Not "It's sharing our bed." Are you sure you haven't got contact magazines mixed up with the rest of your fantasies?'

She leaned back, took aim, and slapped his face hard.

For the second night in succession he slept in the spare room.

Their relationship was fragmenting. They no longer kissed on parting and, more lingeringly, on greeting. She wanted to put the house on the market and move else-where; he wanted to stay. 'I've never run from anything,' he said, 'and I'm not running now.'

'It wouldn't be running.'

'Yes, it would. This is a challenge.'

'Challenge? What are you fighting?'

'I'm fighting your obsession that there's something

supernatural afoot. That's what I'm fighting.'

'I see. So I'm nutty, and you're the reasonable man who has an answer for everything.'

'My reasonableness is wearing distinctly thin.'

'Good. You might with luck become human.'

They were in the kitchen. She had come home early, prepared and eaten a meal. He had boiled an egg and toasted a slice of bread for himself. They were clearing up the remains.

'In your vocabulary,' he said with restrained venom, 'being human means being neurotic. With luck I might become neurotic. That's what you're really saying.'

'Okay, so I'm neurotic, but I'm human, and that's better than being a plastic money-sucker, obsessed by selling techniques. Advertising? How parasitic can you get!'

He clapped his hands; a slow hand-clap. 'Let's hear it for the denigrators,' he said. 'Let's hear it for the parasites who live off parasites.'

His clapping hands were echoed by a rhythmic scratching at the back door.

'This is the bloody end,' he shouted and rushed to the door.

He flung it open. Outside there was a mongrel pup, shivering and cold. It gave a timid whimper.

Jill rushed forward. 'Look at it. I'll bet the poor little thing has been wandering.' She picked up the pup and cuddled it. And she gave her husband a look as if daring him to take it from her arms. 'He's like a little bundle of rags,' she said.

The cutting exchange of words was forgotten. He said, 'I'm damned. So there is a dog.'

'Poor thing. You can feel his ribs. He wants something to eat.'

It was an effort but he managed to say, 'Have you still got those biscuits?'

She gave a sweet smile, a smile he hadn't seen for some time. 'I think he needs something lighter than that. His tummy won't take biscuits. I'll heat up some milk and chop up a bit of steak . . . A bundle of rags,' she mused. 'We'll call you Ragsie.'

She seemed to have taken it for granted that they would keep the pup. With it still in her arms she kissed her husband.

Reconciliation followed that night.

The pup slept peacefully on an old mat in the kitchen.

During the following year the pup grew into a huge ungainly dog, and it followed Jill everywhere. For a while she and Clive vied for its attention but in the end he gave up. It was her dog. She was the one who took it on long walks, fed it, and took it to the vet.

The strange disturbances which had occurred before the advent of the dog were hardly ever mentioned. Clive was fairly certain that in some way these had been engineered by the anti-vivisection protest group but in recent months Jill's company had evolved new methods of testing their products which did not involve animal experiments and the protesters had faded away.

But he became increasingly irritated by the slave-like devotion of Ragsie to its mistress, and her undisguised affection for it. When he had to go away for a week on business he returned to find that it had been allowed to sleep in the bedroom in his absence. 'To keep me company,' she explained.

'Well, I'm back now. He can go back to the kitchen.'

'Why should he? He can sleep on my end of the bed. You won't have your beauty sleep spoiled.'

'I'm not sharing my bed with a dog. I'm not saying anything about being kinky – I'm keeping an open mind on that score – but it's downright unhygienic.'

A fierce quarrel followed which ended with him sleeping in the spare room and the dog sleeping beside her on the bed.

In an attempt to make amends, and because he didn't want to spend any more time in the spare room, Clive got up early and brought her a tray of tea and toast in bed.

The dog rose to its haunches and bared its teeth in a snarl as he entered the room. It only growlingly subsided when Jill, in her sternest voice, commanded, 'Down!' But it watched Clive with unblinking amber eyes and its muzzle crinkled whenever he came too close to its mistress.

Keeping his voice unemotional and his face expressionless Clive said, 'This is ridiculous. I can't come into my own bedroom now.'

'Yes, you can.' She smiled reassuringly. 'It's sudden movements in my direction he doesn't like. In the dog-world it's called "protective aggression".'

'Jill, can't you see it's not exactly usual for a wife to have protective aggression used against her husband when he isn't, by any stretch of the imagination, a wife-beater.'

She laughed; a pretty and natural sound. The dog cocked its head in her direction. 'Don't be silly. You can't expect Ragsie to know things like that. You know it, and I know it, but for heaven's sake be reasonable, how can Ragsie know it?'

'Ragsie,' he echoed bitterly. 'You and me – and Ragsie makes three. Great.' He moved towards the door. 'Excuse me, I want to go to the bathroom. I need to puke.'

It wasn't long after this incident that Jill complained of not feeling well. She had stomach pains and decided to take the day off from work.

Her condition didn't improve and Clive suggested that they called a doctor.

'I'll be all right,' she replied. 'It's just a bug. I'll be okay in no time.'

195

He went off to his office.

Two evenings later he telephoned a close friend.

'Mark? Is that you?... Jill's left. Yes, left. No note. Nothing. Well, she wasn't in last night or tonight. She's gone and taken the bloody dog with her ... Yes, I shall if she doesn't come back tonight... I'm beginning to wonder if she wasn't pretending to be ill so that she could have an excuse to stay at home and make her own arrangements while I was out of the way... What would you do then?... Oh, sure. Carry on as normal is easier said than done ...'

That weekend to occupy himself with physical labour and to avoid thinking about his missing wife he began building a small wall at the back of the house.

Weeks went by and the police, after making enquiries, were unable to help. Clive spent as much time as possible at his job and in his spare time he laid bricks. It was an occupation he found soothing, and he needed peace of mind. Among other things, he sealed up the hearth again, plastered over the brickwork, and so restored the room to its former state.

Jill never returned. Eventually he put up the house for sale and moved away. Shortly after this he sold his share in the advertising agency to his partner. He then joined an agency in New York where he had many business contacts.

The married couple who purchased his house were happy there. One hard winter they decided to unbrick the fireplace in their lounge. 'It would be nice,' the wife had said, 'to have a log fire.' She gave a winsome smile. 'Just think of it. The two of us. A soft rug. No lights on, just the light of a blazing fire.'

A builder removed plaster and brickwork. He found a crate. When he prised it open he found the skeletons of a woman and a large dog.

196

John Wainwright

TOUCHÉ

Arsenic seemed the answer. At first I'd had reservations – after all, the Sedden cock-up, not to mention all the other old poison trials, have tended to give arsenic a bad name – but a gentle mull through Glaister's *Medical Jurisprudence and Toxicology* at the local library had shooed away any misconceptions. The trick, it seemed, was not to shovel it into the victim. Bit at a time was the knack; bit at a time, which caused tummy trouble which, in turn, was diagnosed as gastro-intestinal irritation which, as the arsenic was slowly fed into the patient, gradually worsened until . . . Bingo! One Death Certificate, issued and signed by a slightly worried medic, coming up. No need for an inquest, no need for a post mortem. A quick telephone message to an obliging undertaker, a short but appropriate waffle by some cleric, an opening of closed curtains, and up the crematorium chimney she goes. One more shop-soiled wife neatly disposed of.

Not, of course, that she knew – knew that *I* knew she was shop-soiled, if you see what I mean. I wasn't supposed to know. I was supposed to be the silly ass who stayed at home and kept an eye on the cat on the third Monday of every month, while Mary trotted along to the Arts and Crafts Centre to learn the mysteries of petit point, or some similar feminine frivolity. "My night out". That's what she used to call it. It was, too, but I doubt that she learned much about petit point.

They say – the self-styled wiseacres, who profess to know all about these things – they say the partner is the last person to know in this sort of situation. For the record, and as someone with personal experience, the partner is one of the *first* people to know. That sparkle in the eye, as the Monday approached. That spring in the step when she arrived home. All that tootsie-tootsie business a few days before and a few days after. One would have to be a complete idiot not to suspect, and suspicion is the first tentative step towards certainty.

At first – when I first realised I was being quietly cuckolded – I was shocked. Nothing to do with "manhood" or "virility", let me hasten to say. I pride myself on being more civilised than to place brute emotions very high on my list of priorities. It just seemed (shall we say) rather thoughtless of her and a poor return for the quiet, comparatively prosperous life-style I'd given her. Twenty-five years of comfort deserved something better. Something a little less sordid.

And she had been comfortable. Spoiled even. As manager at an important branch of one of the larger high street banks I'd enjoyed a very handsome salary. I'd invested wisely. I'd paced my life to speed and expenditure well within my means and when, rather late in life, I'd married I'd known that my wife need have no fiscal worries.

Even after the heart attack, the money had been sufficient. More than sufficient. A good, index-linked pension, the income from my investments . . . more than sufficient. I'd no vices; I didn't drink, I didn't smoke, I didn't gamble. Indeed, without being immodest, I estimated myself as being something of a model husband, and Mary as being a very fortunate wife.

Thus, I stroked Felix, the doctored tom who had taken the place of children in our life, stared at the good Welsh coal blazing in the hearth and murmured, 'Arsenic, I think, old boy. Slowly, but surely . . . with arsenic.'

And Felix purred his approval and nestled more comfortably on my lap.

The problem . . . to obtain the poison. Amateur though I was in this gentle art of murder, I was sensible of the stupid mistakes made by others in the past. I wanted no Poison Register. I wanted no signature of mine – not even a false signature – linked with the purchase of arsenic. It seemed, therefore, that Doctor Evans might assist a little.

Evans and I had become rather more than doctor and patient since Mary and I had taken up residence in the tiny cottage overlooking the bay on the Welsh coast. Evans (as if it needs emphasising) was a Welshman but, almost by nature of his calling, an educated Welshman. His interests ranged beyond eisteddfods and male voice choirs. He could converse, with moderate authority, upon many things. Books, for example. Like all Welshmen he was, of course, besotted by the adjectival ramblings of Dylan Thomas but, that apart, he was able to argue the merits and demerits of other great (and to me greater) writers. He'd travelled a little, too. Mainly on the continent of Europe, but on two occasions he'd crossed the Atlantic; once to America, once to Canada.

I think the beauty of the man as an acquaintance was the fact that he knew how to listen. He knew the value of silence, and had the good manners to give due credence to opinions other than those he held himself. On the other hand, he could argue well, without being dogmatic. He was a pleasant, occasional companion then and, as it was necessary for me to collect "repeat prescriptions" from the tiny dispensary attached to his surgery, I almost invariably made an appointment to see him about once a month, for a check-up and for some moderately amusing conversation.

199

I brought up the subject of rats.

'You have a cat,' he said.

'Felix?' I smiled. 'He's fat and lazy. Only hungry cats go for rats.'

'The local pest man,' he suggested.

'I'd thought of him.' I frowned. 'Before we came here, we had the same trouble. The local authority sent out their so-called expert. He put something down.'

'Something for them to eat?'

'They enjoyed it. As far as I could see, it didn't even make them ill.'

'You need poison,' he said.

And he'd mouthed the word first. "Poison". It had been absurdly easy. I'd steered the conversation along certain lines and Evans had made the first move. A little like chess; a skilfully positioned pawn, and he'd been obliged to bring his queen out into the open.

'I don't know much about poisons,' I murmured.

'Something to mix with bran,' he suggested. 'They like bran.'

'Where do I get it?' I asked innocently. 'Some sort of poison, I mean.'

'Something from the dispensary.' He ran his fingers through the thickness of his long, iron-grey hair. 'Something a little more deadly than the branded stuff. We'll have *something*.'

I followed him from the surgery. He closed the dispensary door, against the curious eyes of a handful of locals sitting in the waiting room, then he unlocked the poison cupboard. He ran his hands along the dark-tinted bottles and the screw-topped jars.

'Trichloride of antimony,' he mused, then shook his head and added, 'No, I think not. They'd sniff it. It burns, too. One nibble, and they'd be away. Something – lemme see – something a bit long-winded. Wouldn't you think?'

'You're the expert,' I said gently.

'Aye. Something like this.'

He lifted one of the jars from the cupboard. Printed on a label on the jar's side was the word Arsenic.

As he unscrewed the top, he said, 'Delayed action, see? Mix it with bran. A bit of corn, perhaps. Something they like. Don't be stingy. They won't taste the stuff. A good old feed, then they're away and you're rid of them. That's what you want, eh?'

'If you think so,' I nodded.

He unfolded a small white bag then, with a tiny scoop, he took powder from the jar and almost filled the bag. He screwed the top back on to the jar, returned the jar to the cupboard and re-locked the door. He folded the top of the bag neatly, then secured the fold with a tiny strip of Sellotape.

As he handed me the bag he grinned and said, 'Do the trick, eh?'

'I hope so.'

'Got your own prescription, have you?'

'Thank you.' I patted my jacket pocket, into which I'd dropped my repeat prescription of capsules. I put the tiny bag of arsenic in the other pocket of my jacket, and added, 'I hope it's effective.'

'Oh, it will be. It will be,' he smiled. 'Let me know how things go.'

Before I returned to the cottage I visited the library, and once more checked the information in Glaister's textbook. Grains, it would seem, was the measure, and each ounce weight of arsenic contained 437 grains. The smallest fatal dose recorded was a mere two grains, but on the other hand 230 grains had been swallowed by a would-be suicide . . . and she'd recovered. Arsenic, it would seem, could play peculiar tricks. The textbook didn't say so in as

201

many words but, obviously, each person **had a** private threshold and a murderer was left with a slightly hit-and-miss problem as far as any potential victim was concerned.

I tried to equate Mary with this wide margin of mortality. She was almost seven years younger than myself. Healthy; at times disgustingly healthy. Since our marriage she hadn't suffered a single serious illness. She was active; with the occasional assistance of one of the local unemployed manual workers – a man in his mid-thirties – she'd turned slightly more than an acre of scrub and weed into a good garden, with a lawn, flower beds and a vegetable patch large enough to keep us (and, I have little doubt, the local man who helped) in greenstuff all the year round.

In short, she was as strong as a horse, and I was glad that Evans had been liberal with the arsenic. Around two ounces, at a rough estimate. Eight hundred grains, and on reflection I decided I might *need* it all.

I concentrated upon Glaister's words of wisdom.

Arsenic, it seemed, was very insoluble in cold water. On the other hand, up to a hundred grains could be mixed with cocoa, milk and boiling water and, until that mixture cooled it remained undetectable. No taste, no smell and, until the temperature dropped to below tepid, no curdling of the milk.

We must, I reminded myself, change our routine slightly. We must have a beaker of hot cocoa before we turned in.

The local man – the man who helped with the garden – was there when I arrived home. He was presumably helping, or had *been* helping. He was pushing his arms through the sleeves of his jacket, as I climbed from the car, and Mary was with him and they were both laughing at some private joke.

He waved to me, as he made for the gate at the rear, and I heard Mary call, 'I'll see you tomorrow, David.'

'I'll be here, missus.' Then he was out of the gate and hidden by the tall, copper-beech hedge.

"David"? Not "Mr Morgan". It rankled a little. Employees – and Morgan was an employee whether or not he notified the authorities of the amount I paid him each week – shouldn't be addressed by their first names. Nor should they be allowed to share private jokes with people who paid them. It made for too much intimacy . . . and the work suffered.

As I reached Mary, I said, 'Something funny?'

'What?' She was still smiling as she turned and answered my question by asking one.

'You and Morgan,' I said gently.

'It was something he said.'

'A joke, you mean?'

'No. A turn of phrase. The Welsh have their own way of saying things.'

'You shouldn't be so friendly,' I chided.

'What?' The smile disappeared.

'We employ him.' I pressed the point. 'He'll laugh. He'll talk. Whilever he's laughing and talking, he's not working.'

'He's a good worker.' Suddenly she was defending the man. 'He's strong. He's willing. He'll do anything I ask.'

'Probably.' I nodded thoughtfully. 'Probably he will.'

She frowned at me and said, 'You don't like him.'

It was an accusation; in its own way a deliberate throwing down of an invisible gauntlet.

'I like people I pay to get on with their work,' I said. 'Is that unreasonable?'

'Look, I was only . . .'

'I know,' I interrupted. 'Laughing at his turn of phrase.'

I turned and left her; walked into the house and into my study. I locked the arsenic away in the bottom drawer of my roll-topped desk.

It was as near as we'd ever been to having an argument. I refused to argue . . . with anybody. Over the years I'd taught myself never to lose my temper. Only fools and oafs lose their tempers. In hospital, I voiced this personal opinion to one of the medics and he'd smiled, condescendingly, and suggested that that might have triggered off the heart attack. Bottling it up. Holding it down.

'A man needs to blow the roof occasionally. It's good for him physically, as well as mentally.'

I disagreed. Profoundly. But – again – I wouldn't argue.

Having locked the arsenic away, I took a few deep breaths. One of my tricks; after about the sixth breath my anger dissipated, and I was able to leave the study for the dining room in a perfectly calm frame of mind.

Mary acted as if nothing was amiss. As if I hadn't caught Morgan and her in some private joke. As if she was the perfect wife I'd once thought her to be.

I recall we had trout for the evening meal; we had trout, therefore it must have been a Friday. She was a good cook – that to her credit – and I congratulated her upon both the preparation and the presentation of the meal. Then, having cleared the table, she went into the living room to watch television while I returned to my study on the pretence of reading the rest of the day's newspaper.

In fact, to give more careful thought as to the means and pace of the killing. I took the arsenic from the desk drawer and examined it closely. It was near-white and granular; less coarse then sugar, but perhaps not as finely ground as salt. I rubbed it – just a small pinch of it – between my thumb and forefinger. I even contemplated touching my tongue with a few grains, then had second thoughts. It was, after all, the "classic" poison. Glaister had written that it was almost insoluble in cold water, but much more soluble in a warm drink. I mused about its possible solubility in wine; it was, after all, a very ancient poison – a poison which, in its own way, had determined the course of history – and hot bedtime drinks were a comparatively modern innovation.

I even contemplated a small experiment – with wine, I mean – but dismissed the idea. I was, after all, not a scientist. What I did – whatever I did – would, almost of necessity, be clumsy and inconclusive. No, I had the means with which quietly to dispose of a faithless wife. That was all I needed. The sensible thing was to proceed with caution until what I required was accomplished.

I lighted a cigar – the one cigar I allowed myself each day – then took a box of tissues from a drawer of the desk and set about the task of measuring out the dosage. I quartered each tissue with my penknife, then dipped the tip of the penknife into the arsenic and dropped the tiny measurement on to a quarter of a tissue. When I had sixteen tiny piles of arsenic, I closed the bag, put away the penknife and made sixteen small screws of the poison. Then I locked screws and bag in the desk drawer, settled back in my swivel chair and enjoyed what remained of my cigar.

To put caution before haste. That seemed the sensible thing to do. I therefore waited. I continued my usual daily routine; a quiet, almost monotonous life while at the same time noting things which had previously slipped my notice.

That minute for minute each day he came, Mary spent more time with Morgan than she did with me. Had I felt so disposed I might have been aggrieved, but over the years I'd grown to value solitude. I was not, therefore, unduly displeased. Merely curious; one might almost say morbidly curious. Morbid because gradually – almost against my will – I was forced to acknowledge that the man Morgan was Mary's debauchee. Such a realisation!

Mary, the woman I'd taught to have taste and decorum, lowering her standards to indulge in an affair with an out-of-work, odd-job man.

And yet, in a way, amusing. I sometimes watched them from the window of my study. Saw them enter the tiny greenhouse and become hidden behind the vine and the pot plants. I would time them sometimes. Five minutes — ten minutes — sometimes even a quarter of an hour. It was only a small greenhouse; it wasn't large enough to hold enough horticultural specimens to keep them either occupied or interested for such a length of time. Kissing, perhaps. Whispering sweet stupidities to each other. Fondling each other, perhaps. A darkness seemed to enter my mind as mental pictures built up and added to my disgust.

And yet amusing . . . albeit an amusement with black edges.

Jealousy? Please, I beg you, credit me with the ability to control such a base emotion as jealousy. Of what should I have been jealous? Another man's genitals? No, whatever else, not jealousy. And yet, anger. Yes, anger was there, as much as I could allow myself.

The heart condition precluded me from over-excitement. The warning from the medics had been quite specific. No over-excitement of any sort, otherwise . . .

Therefore I quite deliberately controlled my anger. And yet I had cause to be angry. Over the years I had surrounded myself with objects of interest, objects of beauty, objects of a cultural nature. Books, ornaments, furniture. Even this cottage; it was in its original — what one might call "mint" — condition and, to the best of my not inconsiderable knowledge, everything about it was genuine. I appreciated these things. I valued them beyond price. The same, I suppose, with Mary. Had some vandal defaced the walls or the beams of my cottage

– smashed one of my porcelain miniatures – fouled upon the Persian carpet which covered the floor of my study – torn pages from one of my first editions . . . then I would have been angry. The equation could be carried forward to my wife.

Anger, then, and not a little mystification. The man was an oaf. He laughed too much, and too loudly to be anything other than an oaf. And Mary. She was some few years younger than I, but she was no longer *young*. She was well past the "flighty" stage. She could, had she so wished (had she had the sense I'd once thought she had) have settled back to a tranquil, well-mannered life. A quiet life. A civilised life. But instead . . .

I gave her two more Mondays. Two more "nights out". Two more pretended visits to the Arts and Crafts Centre. It seemed wise so to do. I wanted no immediate mental connection between the obtaining of the arsenic and her "tummy upset". During this period I visited Evans's surgery a couple of times for my own "repeat prescription" and, once, he asked about the rats. A mere passing reference. I assured him that they no longer posed a problem, without actually naming the supposed reason for their disappearance, and he was obviously satisfied. I also introduced the habit of having a nightcap, immediately prior to our retiring. Hot cocoa. A beaker each, and I was slightly amused at Mary's enjoyment of this hot-drink end to each day.

I made the cocoa. Again this was necessary and I gave as my excuse that Mary had had a "busy day" and that all she need do was relax in her armchair while I brewed the last drink of the day.

The first introduction of a twist of arsenic caused me some small anxiety. I watched her as she sipped, then drained, the poisoned drink. She made no remark;

Glaister, it seemed, was right. And the next morning she complained of an upset stomach which had necessitated her going to the bathroom twice, during the night.

'You should have called me,' I said sympathetically.

'No . . . it must have been something I ate.'

'You look a little off colour,' I ventured.

'Not really.'

'Should I call Doctor Evans?'

'Good heavens, no.' She suddenly burst into a quiet titter. I looked puzzled.

' "Heavens", "Evans",' she explained. 'It sounds so funny.'

"Funny"! That hurt me. It annoyed me. The stupid woman was being poisoned and, even accepting the fact that she didn't *know* she was being poisoned, it was an inappropriate time for making silly puns.

Perhaps that was something else they enjoyed together; my wife and Morgan. Perhaps they giggled and laughed as they made infantile play upon words. Puns, limericks, the snide double entendre beloved of low-class comedians leave me unmoved. Unlike Morgan, I was not a muscle-bound, hearty type. I treasured individualism. I loathed crowds; massed humanity where everybody is, almost of necessity, reduced to a single lowest common denominator . . . the level of the most foolish.

She must be taught to differentiate between humour and stupidity.

That night I gave her another twist of poison.

I thought I'd gone too far. She really was ill. At about midnight she knocked on my bedroom door and, having tied a dressing-gown over my pyjamas, I opened the door and she almost collapsed in my arms.

'God! I feel awful,' she whispered.

208

'Stomach trouble?' I enquired solicitously.

'I'm bringing up blood,' she moaned.

I helped her back to her bedroom, but she refused to lie down. Instead, she sprawled in a wicker armchair and made tiny mewing noises.

'Shall I telephone the doctor?' I asked.

'No . . . not yet,' she breathed.

'Not *yet?*'

'When it's light. Ask him to call on his rounds.'

'Do you think we should wait?'

She managed a ghost of a smile and said, 'I'm not *dying,* dear.'

But she *was* . . . and, just for a moment, I almost weakened and hoped she wasn't.

Doctor Evans called on his morning round and diagnosed "stomach trouble".

In the lounge, and out of earshot of my wife, he was more specific.

He said, 'Some sort of gut spasm, I think. Acute dyspepsia, perhaps. Keep her in bed. Keep her warm. Lots of warm drinks. I'll call in this evening with an anti-cholinergic preparation.'

'You don't think it's serious?' I questioned with mock-anxiety.

'No, no.' He smiled. 'She'll be her old self in a week or two.'

The next three weeks were a little trying. I abhor illness and especially messy illness. I abhor it in myself and it nauseates me in others. It was, therefore, not a happy period.

I fed the arsenic slowly – more slowly than on the first two occasions – and, gradually, I grew to be something of a self-educated expert. Indeed, and to give the required effect, I withheld the poison for short periods and Mary began to think she was recovering ... then, having achieved this plateau of apparent recovery, I re-started the poisoning and progressed in what I thought was a normal, but worsening, stomach illness.

Doctor Evans called, morning and evening. Sometimes he was optimistic. Sometimes not. As for Mary, had she not been the faithless wife she was, I might have pitied her. Her general malaise grew more pronounced. She refused food, other than the hot drinks and the medicine prescribed by Doctor Evans. There was a great deal of vomiting, and she began to complain of numbness in her hands and feet. For the last week, or thereabouts, I had to assist her to the bathroom; she'd lost weight and she wobbled as if under the influence of drink.

Just the once, Morgan asked about her health. Was "the missus getting better"? I took him to her bedroom, and let him see for himself. I stood in the background and watched the two of them stare, rather stupidly, at each other. Morgan didn't know what to do with his hands. I thought I detected the glint of tears in Mary's eyes. I will not go as far as to say that I was gratified but, nevertheless, their obvious misery gave me a sense of slight satisfaction.

Downstairs Morgan muttered, 'She's in a bad way, mister.'

'It would seem so.'

'If – if there's anything *I* can do.'

'Think of her.' I deliberately kept my voice expressionless.

'That I will.'

'With your usual affection.'

'Aye.' He bobbed his head. 'I reckon she's one of the nicest people I've ever met.'

The end came on a Saturday evening. Doctor Evans had called, he'd examined her, then returned to the lounge, where I'd offered him a whisky. We sat in armchairs and talked.

Quite suddenly, at the end of a pause in our conversation, he said, 'The arsenic.'

'The arsenic?' I kept my voice steady, and made his remark into a question.

'I've been checking my records. You didn't sign for it. My mistake . . . I should have reminded you.'

'Oh!' I smiled.

'Did you need all of it?' he asked, pleasantly.

'No. I – er – the rats have all disappeared.'

'Good.' He opened his bag, fingered the contents into a more tidy order then, without looking up, added, 'I'll take what you have left. We'll estimate how much you've used, then you can sign for it when you call at the surgery.'

'I've used very little,' I said. 'Hardly any.'

'Good.'

'I'll bring it. It's locked away in my desk. For safety purposes.'

I went to the study, unlocked my desk and shook the contents of the remaining twists back into the bag. I was pleasantly surprised at how little arsenic I had, in fact, used. I was tempted to keep one, perhaps two, twists back, but thought better of it. The poison *was* better out of the way; I contemplated no awkward questions, but with the arsenic back in Doctor Evans's poison cupboard, plus the fact that the register hadn't been signed, it was a sort of "fail safe" situation. As for Mary. Supposing she improved – supposing her system could take the arsenic I'd fed into it – that wasn't *too* important. I'd read, somewhere, that finely ground glass was also a very effective poison.

Doctor Evans was still sipping his whisky when I returned to the lounge. He took the arsenic and, without even examining it, tucked it away in his bag.

Then he said, 'I think you'd better take one of your capsules.'

'Why? I've already taken one today.'

'Take a second,' he insisted. 'What I'm going to say may come as a shock.'

I could guess what he was going to say. Nevertheless, the play-acting had to be continued, therefore I walked to the side-table, unscrewed the top of the bottle I kept there, and dutifully swallowed a capsule.

'Sit down,' he said quietly.

I sat down.

He hesitated a moment then in a gentle voice said, 'She won't last the night out.'

'Oh!' I pretended shock, mixed with horror. 'I didn't realise she was as ill as . . .'

'At an educated guess, she'll be dead within two hours. Three at the most.'

'That's – that's very distressing.'

'After all the arsenic *you've* been feeding into her?'

This time the question – accompanied, as it was, with the slow smile and the raised eyebrow – *did* shock me. I moistened my lips and waited.

'You're not denying it,' he observed quietly.

'Let us assume . . .' I began.

'We haven't time for assumptions.'

The time for pretence had ended and in a cold, accusing voice, I said, '*You* provided the arsenic.'

'What arsenic?' he asked, innocently. 'I've no record of arsenic having been taken from the poison cupboard.'

'In that case . . .'

'Let me explain.' He made a tiny gesture for silence, with his right hand. 'When a happily married and respected member of a community – like myself – is suddenly confronted by a not-too-young, but very attractive woman – like your wife – things tend to happen. Clandestine meetings in hotel bedrooms . . . that sort of thing.'

'So it was *you*. Not Morgan.'

'Who's Morgan?'

'He's our . . . It doesn't matter.'

'Things happen.' He stood up and strolled to the side-table as he continued. 'Then – after a while – those things become something of a nuisance. Something of a danger.' He picked up the bottle of capsules and returned to his chair. Still talking. 'The novelty wears off, but what can that happily married, respected member of the community do? How can he feel *absolutely* safe?' He unscrewed the top of the bottle and spilled the capsules into the palm of his hand. He continued, 'Unless, of course, the husband of the woman becomes suspicious and decides to poison her. Unless, of course, the respected member of the community happens to be a doctor . . . and able to provide the poison. Then things become ridiculously easy. As their GP in attendance, I can issue a Death Certificate.' From his jacket pocket he produced an envelope and from the envelope he began to feed other capsules into the bottle. '*Two* Death Certificates. One for the woman who died as a result of . . . "something to do with the stomach". I have a dozen choices, none of which will be contested. One for the man – a man with a dicky heart – who, having found his dead wife, collapsed and died.'

'I've – I've no intention of . . .'

'You've no option.' He slid the capsules from his palm into the empty envelope, looked up and smiled. 'I must hurry,' he said, very conversationally. 'We haven't much time. But tomorrow morning I'll call round. I shall not be able to make myself heard, of course. The door will be locked – I'll drop the latch-lock on my way out – and the police will have to break in. You'll both be dead.' He held up my bottle, containing the capsules. 'These capsules . . . very handy. For example, you've just swallowed enough potassium cyanide to kill a horse. And when the capsule melts . . .'

He snapped his fingers and chuckled.

'How – how long?' I breathed.

'Not long,' he said cheerfully. 'Seconds, that's all . . . and you won't feel a thing.'

I stared at him.

I was still staring at him, when the capsule melted. Staring . . . but not *seeing*.

Margaret Yorke

A TIME FOR INDULGENCE

Looking in the mirror, I see a white, fat face – pale eyes,
sparse brows, which now I pencil over darkly. My lips are
a bright bow of painted pink. My hand shakes as I apply
mascara to my scanty lashes. I add rouge over my cheek-
bones and powder the whole. My mask is on for the day.

In the bathroom adjoining our hotel room, my husband
is taking his morning bath. The water slurps and splashes.
He will be some time yet; the ritual toilet lasts for over an
hour as first he shaves his jowly chin, then soaps his
scrawny body with its grizzled hair.

Last night, in the four poster bed in this hotel bedroom,
my husband used me. He plunged and groaned, trying to
make of me a mustang to meet his bucking. Above us, the
canopy stretched, silent witness of intimate encounter.
Later, in sleep, he pushed me away, taking for himself the
centre of the dipping bed, snoring heavily. When I tried to
win for myself enough space to find some rest, he lashed
out at me with a flailing arm. At last I took my pillow to
the armchair and dozed a little. This morning my feet and
ankles are sadly swollen.

Why not twin beds, you ask.

My husband frequently, even now, demands his rights,
and insists they remain within reach. A holiday, he has
said, is a time for indulgence.

I am wearing my white linen sundress, which exposes

my flabby white arms and much of my heavy shoulders, though wide straps conceal my underwear. My husband has always liked me to be dressed in white, so to please him I seldom wear colours. I will go down to the terrace and sit there in the sunshine, waiting until he comes downstairs, for I must not go into breakfast without him. You would expect me to have no appetite after such a night, but I am constantly hungry. At the thought of coffee, hot toast, bacon and egg, saliva runs in my mouth.

While I wait, others enter the hotel dining-room: the slender, pale girl with the fine dark hair that falls to her shoulders, and her tall young husband with the full soft lower lip. His hand guides her ahead of him, possessively touching her back, and she turns to smile intimately at him.

I think of a day in Venice: of a pale slender girl in a full-skirted muslin dress sprigged with small flowers and with a wide-brimmed hat on her dark hair, her husband's hand firm on her elbow as they cross the Piazza San Marco: myself.

He always took thought for me. In those first years before the war a daily maid helped with the heavier work in our small house in Wimbledon. I saw that all ran smoothly to please my husband, as was my duty. The silver shone with polishing; the furniture gleamed with beeswax; tasty, nourishing meals were punctually served. For a time I went to a cookery school, to learn basic methods, and embellished these by advice from books whose complicated recipes I followed with increasing success. We gave little dinners for some of my husband's friends. He would give me a bouquet of flowers on the day of such a dinner; the guests, when he brought it to their notice, thought it a charming thing to do.

Our intimate moments were troubling to me. I had

216

none of the knowledge girls seem to acquire so easily these days, and I was too timid to ask advice from other young women; such matters could not be mentioned to a mere acquaintance and I had no close female friend, nor a sister; my mother was dead. A husband to provide for her was what every girl hoped for then; a job was a stop-gap until marriage was safely arranged, and to remain unmarried was to be labelled a social failure. Careers were for the few, who were thought eccentric and unwomanly. How different things are today! I envy modern girls their independence. Now no woman need pay for her keep in a manner that degrades her.

For years I imagined that all women felt as I did about these things. Then came the war.

My husband, who worked in a bank (I had met him there, paying in money for the draper in whose shop I was employed as cashier), had earlier joined the territorial army; he enjoyed their manoeuvres and meetings, and looked well in his uniform. I was pleased that he had this interest and never minded that it took him away from home for hours, sometimes for days; for me, these intervals brought blessed rest. He was called up even before war was declared, and was soon in France, a commissioned officer. I felt proud.

In the collapse of 1940 he was taken prisoner, and he spent the rest of the war in various camps in Germany.

Left alone, childless, I let the house for the duration of the war and joined the ATS. At first I worked as a cook, for this was my only skill, but when I found that army food, cooked in bulk, could never resemble the tempting dishes I had been used to concocting for my husband's pleasure, I applied to become a driver and was accepted for training. I reasoned that this work, carried on outdoors and often alone in a car or lorry, would offer relief from the pressures of noise and constant company which I found trying. I was not good at mixing, and was older than many of the other girls.

I was a conscientious pupil and was soon proficient at the wheel, taught by a brisk middle-aged sergeant with a red face and a surprising amount of patience. I learned some mechanics, and took pride in maintaining my vehicle in efficient order. For the next five years I drove lorries round Britain to gun sites and supply depots.

I wrote regularly to my husband and arranged for parcels to be sent to him. He replied at intervals, terse notes with requests for things he wanted, but I knew his letters would be read and censored and expected nothing more. He studied for a law degree while he was in the camp, but he failed his examinations. He did not try to escape. Escapers, he said when at last he came home, were a nuisance to those who had settled down to a course of study in an effort to profit from their captivity. He blamed his examination failure on the fact that he was obliged to give background help to would-be escapers, acting as look-out and so on, which disturbed his studies.

Because I was married, I did not go out on 'dates' like the other girls. In my spare time I knitted warm garments for my husband and for other service men. I became a good knitter and found it peaceful employment, though I don't knit now. I went to the cinema often; there were plenty of good films to see then. Sometimes I went to concerts; I still listen to them on the radio if my husband is not in the house; he does not like music.

I was content. It was as though my life in Wimbledon with my husband had never been. I did not look ahead.

I was given a stripe, and then a second; as a responsible married woman I was an obvious candidate for an eventual sergeant's stripe, even a commission, but I never rose higher. I was not flighty, likely to get into trouble, like so many girls. Their conversation, as they talked about their amorous adventures, often shocked me; it surprised me, too, describing pleasure they obtained from experiences that would have been only distasteful to me.

Then, one fine warm night, walking back to the billets with one of the men who helped maintain our vehicles, everything changed. He suddenly slid his arm round me in the darkness, turned me to face him, and kissed my lips. Holding me close to him, he remarked that I was a fine girl, always cheerful, though my husband had been so long in the prison camp and wasn't I missing him?

I was so astonished by his action that I did not push him away at once. Nor did I connect what had happened with the encounters I had had with my husband. The soldier's lips were soft and warm. He kissed me again, his battle-dress rough against my hands which, to my amazement, were holding him. He led me away to a far corner of a field and undid my jacket, then my shirt. What followed was unimaginable bliss. I no more thought of protesting than I would have of refusing to take my vehicle out when ordered. We spent a long time together in that field, but it never happened between us again; he was posted away soon afterwards and I did not hear from him at all. But I remembered.

I did not become pregnant, but now I understood the other girls better and was kinder to them.

The war ended and my husband came home. We returned to Wimbledon. I hoped that things would be different between us, more as they had been with the soldier, but nothing was altered: if anything, matters were worse than before, for now I knew the difference. One night I wept, and in the end, when he berated me, told him the reason.

He beat me with his army belt, then used me again, violently and viciously.

'I will never forgive you,' he said. 'Behaving loosely,

while I was behind the wire suffering for my country and half starved.'

'I know, I know,' I wept. 'I'm sorry.'

His thoughtfulness for me increased after that. Every day he telephoned me at half-past ten, using the office phone. He had not returned to the bank, but was now, after all those years of study, a solicitor's clerk. If I went out shopping, I had to hurry home to receive his call. He rang at odd times during the day, too, and if by chance I was out I had to account for where I was when he came home. Every evening he wanted to know exactly how my day had been spent.

I worked harder than before to ensure that the house was perfectly kept and the meals as good as ever, to afford no further cause for complaint.

I was always tired. The nights were dreadful and I slept little, but each afternoon I dozed off with a comforting box of chocolates beside me. My husband did not know about the chocolates, and I told him I had spent the time reading. He selected books he considered appropriate for me, improving volumes of biography or history, never fiction, bringing them home from the library, but I read few of them for I could not concentrate on their sober contents. I bought magazines, secretly, and paperback romances, which I read with my feet up on the sofa. I had no close friends. I seldom went out to coffee mornings for my husband's morning call made it difficult unless the hostess lived close by. Soon I gave up trying and my few acquaintances dropped away.

Our dinner parties resumed, with my husband's business connections as guests, and again he brought me flowers on the evenings of those days.

'What a good husband,' the guests would purr, made by him to understand what he had done.

When we were invited back, he no longer took me with

220

him but would telephone to say I had a migraine, and must be excused. He would lock up all my shoes in a cup-board then, leaving me only my slippers.

'I'm not letting you go out to behave like a trollop,' he would say.

He would return very late on such nights, elated, and his elation might last for several days. I would lie motion-less in bed, feigning sleep, expectant and afraid, but I would be unmolested. It frightens me now to think of the possible reason for his exalted mood. I shall never know if I am right.

Food was my solace, and soon I grew fat, eating cream cakes at four-thirty with my cup of tea.

Why did I stay?

At times I thought of leaving him, but where could I go and what could I do? I had no money of my own, and no training apart from my ability to cook and to drive most sorts of vehicle. I could not divorce my husband, obliging him to pay me alimony, for it was not he, but I who had committed a matrimonial offence, as he pointed out to me when once I went so far as to pack a small bag and rush to the front door in the middle of the night. He would hunt me down, he said, wherever I went, disgrace me publicly but never let me go. I believed him.

'You are my wife,' he told me sternly. 'You are mine.'

Gradually the desire to escape withered away; I grew resigned, like one in gaol, to my endless sentence. Some-times I would think of that long-ago interlude with the young soldier, whose face had faded by now from my memory; I would murmur his name under my breath, and try to remember the tenderness he had shown me.

Then my husband retired, and the few hours' respite I had had each day were gone. He took up growing orchids, making a success of them, in a large greenhouse which he built in our garden. Each July a neighbour tended it while we went on our annual holiday, always to a different cliff-top hotel at some seaside resort. In the mornings we would walk over the headland, often along hilly, difficult paths, and in the afternoons my husband would swim in the hotel pool while I, in my white sundress, would sit watching him pant splashingly up and down, and rise to hold his towel for him when he emerged.

My husband is old now, but he is still vigorous. I do not enjoy our holidays as I trail after him on our long walks, or pour his tea in hotel lounges. Sometimes I play clock golf with him, or croquet, though I do not care for games.

Last year there was a tragic accident at the place where we were staying. A young girl fell to her death from the cliff top near the hotel. A path led there from the hotel garden, and the girl, a guest in the hotel, had walked that way with her husband after dinner. Her husband – they were on their honeymoon – had returned to the hotel to fetch a coat for her as the night was getting chilly. He left her, he said later, sitting on a rock watching a ship, brilliantly lit, passing on the horizon. They intended to stroll further before going to bed, perhaps down to the shore to seek for shells in the light of the moon. Steps cut from the cliff descended near to where he left his slender, pale wife in her white dress. When he returned, she had vanished. He thought she might have gone down to the beach, and searched there for her, but could find no trace of her.

The girl was dead, dying before the stars went from her eyes.

Were there stars in my eyes after that brief war-time interlude? No one remarked on them at the time.

My husband had kindled nothing in me. His touch was death.

Last year, as that young couple went out into the moon-lit night together, my husband set forth on the walk he

222

took after dinner each evening. He no longer insisted that I accompany him, tittupping over the grass in the high heels he decrees I must wear. I stayed in the hotel lounge, glancing at a magazine. He was not gone long, but said it was time for bed when he returned. His walk had done him good; he was alert, elated, as on his return from dinner party visits without me; and as on those nights, he did not trouble me. We missed the commotion when the distraught young husband returned to the hotel and the search for his missing wife began.

When I washed my husband's shirt the next day, I found a long dark hair clinging to it. I looked at his jacket and saw another there. I brushed the jacket well, not comprehending at the time.

It was only much later that I remembered other accidents at places we had visited. Four years ago a young girl who lived in the neighbouring town – not a guest in the cliff-top hotel – was killed in a fall, and there was another similar case the next year at the place where we stayed. The verdict on those two deaths was misadventure, for too little of the bodies was left, after some weeks' immersion in the sea, to prove anything else. Crabs, I have read, devour human flesh in the ocean. I have never cared for the strong flavour of crab.

I know what he did to each girl before she fell. Perhaps he prevented her screaming by strangling her first. It must always have been so quick.

It is going to happen again.

He has noticed this slender young girl in white with the fine dark hair. I have seen him watching her. It is myself as I was when young, and in his mind he kills me each time he does it, after the violation.

Last year he miscalculated, for the tide did not come up in time to prevent the girl's body being found. The moonlight helped too, and the searchers saw her white dress caught on a rock.

Her young husband was suspected of her murder, but on some detail of evidence not made clear in the papers it was later decided that he was not her attacker. That was when I remembered the hairs on my husband's clothes. We had long since returned to Wimbledon.

That girl last year was the daughter of my lost young soldier lover of a single night. He came to the hotel the next day, a sad man, well into middle age now, a widower, we learned. He was bewildered by what had happened. I would not have recognised him after all those years if I had not heard his name.

I saw him sitting sadly in the garden, and went up to him to express my sorrow over the accident. The girl and her husband had looked so happy, I told him, and he seemed pleased, but, understandably, his manner was abstracted. I asked him if he had been in Lincolnshire during the war, and he looked surprised but said he had. A friend of mine was stationed there, in the ATS, I said, and named myself.

He did not remember.

I will follow my husband tonight when he goes for his evening stroll. I will follow him every night until my chance comes. This year I have a bright, sharp knife in my bag. I brought it with me from my kitchen at home, for my plan was made long ago. I will plunge it into him. But now I must do it before he can attack his next victim, seizing my opportunity to save not only her life but also her young body from his abuse. Somehow I must find enough strength in my poor weak legs to creep up behind him undiscovered, and in my hand for the deed.

Perhaps I will do it tonight.

What happens to me when I have killed my husband does not matter, for I am dead already.